COUGAR TRACKS

Former US Army scout Carroll Cougar desires only to live peacefully on his Twin Creek ranch. Then a letter from the President arrives. Enemy forces plan to assassinate General Crook, and the Army wants Cougar back to take out the threat . . . The old scout has no desire to return to military life. But when he learns that Crook's would-be killer is none other than Solon Reineke, he swiftly saddles up to answer the call of duty. For Reineke is the man who murdered Carlina Polk, a woman Cougar loved . . .

OWEN G. IRONS

COUGAR
TRACKS

Complete and Unabridged

LINFORD
Leicester

First published in Great Britain in 2014 by
Robert Hale Limited
London

First Linford Edition
published 2016
by arrangement with
Robert Hale Limited
London

A catalogue record for this book is available
from the British Library.

ISBN 978–1–4448–2789–7

Published by
F. A. Thorpe (Publishing)
Anstey, Leicestershire

Set by Words & Graphics Ltd.
Anstey, Leicestershire
Printed and bound in Great Britain by
T. J. International Ltd., Padstow, Cornwall

This book is printed on acid-free paper

1

First he yawned, then he shot the one on his left. It was too early for such nonsense, Carroll Cougar thought. The sun was slanting down prettily through the cottonwoods along the creek and the mountains were just drawing their bulk out of the darkness beyond the low meadow. But the Fenners had come hunting for him early.

There were three return shots from near the cabin, but they had no idea where Cougar was, only that he was in the trees. He hated to do it, but it seemed he was going to have to shoot the other two as well. Otherwise there would be no end to this foolishness. The kid was only about nineteen, Cougar reckoned, but the Winchester he carried was full grown.

What they had done was to creep close to the cabin in the hour before dawn and slip across the frosted morning grass, ready to fire at the windows and break the door down if they had to after they had called him out. But Cougar hadn't been there; for many a night now he had been awaiting their coming, sleeping outside on the ground in various places. And this morning when dawn had broken it had brought the guns and scarlet death to the valley.

'All right, Trace,' Cougar muttered to himself as he got to his feet. 'Let's have at it.'

The big man wore no hat. His roughly cut, shaggy hair hung to his shoulders. He tucked the small silver disc he wore on a rawhide thong around his neck inside his faded blue shirt so that it would not catch and reflect the morning sunlight. He moved swiftly but easily, with the grace of a big cat, toward the verge of the cotton-woods. He had already spotted another of them — the one who would die first. The kid had been positioned foolishly on the limb of the big oak near the woodshed, searching for Cougar with narrowed eyes. It was a good way, Cougar thought, for Trace Fenner to get another of his sons killed. But then, Fenner never had been real clever.

All Cougar had wanted when he came back to Texas from the far West was to build a cabin and have room to graze his horses. All Fenner wanted was everything. Even though it was Fenner who had originally sold him the Twin Creek ranch and knew full well the title was good, the water rights inviolable, after Fenner had spent Cougar's cash money he had returned with armed men demanding a section of the Twin Creek water for his cattle. Even then, Cougar had tried to be reasonable with the rancher.

'You can use what you need, Fenner,' Cougar had replied to the crusty rancher, 'just water your steers down-stream from my horses. I don't want my water fouled by your beef.'

'I'll take what I want when I damn

3

well want,' the confident Fenner had snapped. He knew that Cougar was a man living alone, and as big as he was even Carroll Cougar wasn't going to stand against a party of armed men — or so he had thought.

But then, he didn't know Carroll Cougar very well. He should have taken the time to study his man. It would have saved him from a dead son and the impossible situation he now occupied.

The kid in the tree caught sight of Cougar suddenly, yelled out, 'I see him, Dad!' and swung his rifle around to train his sights on the approaching Cougar. The kid was just too slow. Cougar's .56 Spencer bellowed, smoke straggled into the morning-colored sky, and the kid, his mouth open, arms thrown out desperately, toppled from the tree, thudding lifelessly to the damp grass beneath the oak.

'Cougar!' Trace Fenner's voice cracked as hysteria rose in his throat.

'What is it, Trace?' Cougar asked

from the position he had taken up in an old buffalo wallow. 'You ready to make a run for it?'

'Run for it! Why, you bastard, I'm ready to cut your belly open and feed your guts to the buzzards!'

'Well, then,' Cougar replied softly, 'you're welcome to come along and try that as well.'

The day had turned forebodingly silent. The early sunlight slanting through the oak tree mottled the grass there and the dead body upon it. The waft and warp of passing larks formed quick lace against the deep red sky to the east.

Cougar waited.

He caught himself whistling softly under his breath. An old habit. He had been a player in the game of stalking for so many years. He had hoped that now those years were finally gone and that he had come home. Perhaps they would never pass, though — until he was the one who carelessly skylined himself, stepped on one small, dry twig or let metal click against metal, and an enemy with sharper eyes, better hearing than his, won the last bloody roll of the dice.

Fenner was no Apache, no trained scout. He was a cowhand; his boots were heavy and the waiting game wasn't to his liking as the sun grew hotter and slowly creeping beetles moved over the dead flesh of his sons.

Fenner rose up from the long grass with a roar, his eyes wild and red, hair spiked and sweaty, the lever of his Winchester slicking down and back as he fired three times, the bullets harrowing the dark earth around Cougar's prone body.

All was smoke and sudden motion, Fenner's charging, twisting body slinging itself at Cougar as birds scattered into the streaky crimson sky.

Cougar fired once and the three hundred-grain bullet from the .56 Spencer simply detonated bone and tissue as it sawmilled into Fenner's skull. Fenner rolled to one side, the rifle in his hands spinning free, sunlight

6

harsh on the barrel. His legs were lifted into the air and slammed to the earth again. There was a long, vagrant echo following the gunshot and then again there was silence, the breeze sighing once more in the trees as though with relief after the violence of the morning, and Cougar slowly dragged himself to his feet, feeling the perspiration trickle down his throat and back. He toed Fenner's body and walked slowly to the tool shed, put down the rifle and picked up a shovel.

When he emerged from the shed into the blinding sunlight the man on the black horse was there.

The newcomer's hat was low, eyes lost in the umbra of its brim. He had a rifle held loosely in his hand and wore a Colt .44 on his hip. Cougar tensed reflexively and then relaxed, leaning on the shovel as he looked up at the horseman.

'Hello, Carroll,' the inrider said, sheathing his rifle and resting his hands on the pommel of his saddle as he glanced around the yard of the cabin. 'Get them all?'

'I think so, but you never know, do you, Calvin?' Cougar asked, lifting his eyes to the surrounding yellow-green hills.

'No,' Calvin D'Arcy agreed. He too glanced briefly at the hills where shadows played in the canyons and a dozen more killers could be hidden. 'That's just it — you never do know for sure.' D'Arcy had tilted his hat back, revealing sober, thoughtful eyes. He was long, lean, scarred, and trail dusty, his fringe of mustache dark and wind-wayward. He was a dangerous man as Cougar knew full well, and a secretive man appearing and disappearing as the notion struck him.

'How'd you find me?' Cougar asked.

'I just followed the sound of the shots,' D'Arcy said dryly. 'It sounded like a war down here. I thought you might be needing some help. But then the shooting stopped and the last shot sounded like a big Spencer to me. I figured you were the last man standing.'

'That's not what I mean,' Cougar said. 'What are you doing in the area at all? Last I heard you were down on the Cimarron.'

'That was a while back now. I've been looking for you, Cougar. You figured that already.' Then carefully but smoothly D'Arcy swung down from his black horse.

'Do you mind telling me why you wanted to find me, Calvin?' Cougar asked slowly.

'A lot of people want to find you,' D'Arcy answered with a smile. He took his hat off, fingered back his dark hair, and dusted himself off. Cougar didn't like the reply, but he said nothing. 'I'd like to water my horse,' D'Arcy said, lifting a chin toward the well and adjoining water tank, 'if it's all right?'

'You're welcome to it,' Cougar said. 'I'll be in the cabin when you've finished. I guess my work can wait a little while; they don't seem to be going anywhere.'

D'Arcy smiled that enigmatic smile of his, replaced his hat, and watched as the big man walked back toward the cabin, still carrying the shovel. After D'Arcy had unsaddled his horse, watered it, and rubbed the black gelding down, he returned to the cabin, calling out before he stepped up onto the narrow porch where a single low-backed chair rested.

'Come on in!' Cougar called in return to his hail. There was resignation and displeasure in his tone. The day had not begun well and it showed no indication of getting better.

Cougar sat on a reversed chair behind the puncheon table in the low-ceilinged two-room cabin. He had placed his forearms on the table, the sleeves of the faded, checked yellow shirt he had changed into rolled up to reveal long, powerful muscles. He nodded across to the other chair and D'Arcy seated himself, seeing the welcoming bottle of whiskey and pot of coffee Cougar had provided.

D'Arcy placed his trail-dusty hat on the table, reached for the whiskey bottle and splashed some into one of the two blue metal coffee cups. Cougar didn't move except for following D'Arcy's motions with his appraising green-gray eyes. Behind Cougar a mockingbird perched on the window sill and peered in, screeched once, and darted away again on white-banded gray wings.

'I appreciate the hospitality,' D'Arcy said. He drank the two fingers of whiskey in his cup and filled it with coffee, cupped in his hard brown hands. He looked around lazily, seeing the saber on the wall, below it an old .45-70 Springfield rifle, the stained and misshapen cavalry hat, and the new Winchester propped up in the corner, a piece of cloth tucked into its muzzle to protect it from dust.

'You'd better get on with it,' Carroll Cougar said finally, impatiently. 'I've got things to do, Calvin.'

'It's simple, Carroll,' D'Arcy said, helping himself to another splash of liquor, 'they need you back.'

'Who needs me?' Carroll asked, laughing.

'The army,' D'Arcy said from under his unkempt mustache. His eyes locked with Cougar's, finding mockery in them.

'Someone's crazy,' Cougar said with another laugh, sipping at his dark coffee. 'Is it you, D'Arcy?'

'Maybe,' D'Arcy shrugged. 'I never give it much thought — but that's what they want, that's why they sent me to find you for them.'

'Who?' Cougar demanded. The mockery had faded from his eyes to be replaced by steely-edged defiance.

'I just told you — the army wants you back, Carroll.'

'The army can crumple up and blow away,' Cougar said, not with bitterness, but with determination. 'Are they that needful these days that they have to go out and dig up every old gray-haired scout they ever had?'

'I don't see no gray hair on your

head, Cougar,' D'Arcy said. 'Don't you go pretending to me that you're some withered-up, crooked, cracker-barrel codger with your pine box already built.'

'I'm not pretending anything,' Cougar said, laughing again, this time harshly. 'I don't need to pretend, and I don't need or want the army. I said someone was crazy — I was right. But it isn't me. I've found a place to make my stand, Calvin, and I'm content and comfortable with what I've got. Go back and tell whoever sent you that they're crazier than you are.'

He started to rise but D'Arcy unexpectedly put a hand on his forearm. 'Carroll,' D'Arcy said with deep sincerity reflecting in his eyes, 'this is important.'

'Nothing's that important,' Cougar responded.

'Yeah, it is. This is.' D'Arcy took a deep breath and said carefully, 'Let me explain . . . '

'Explain nothing. Don't waste your

time, Calvin. There's nothing the army has that I want. I don't care to sit a saddle in a blizzard with my fingers and toes frostbitten, or in some devil sandstorm with my butt aching, my throat and lungs burning and clogged with smothering dust. I don't want to lie low in some ravine with Comanches sniffing around for me, my stomach empty, bugs crawling up my neck, my ammunition gone. I don't want to stand in a battle line and see my friends shot to pieces, or ride down valiantly waving a saber at the enemy. I don't want any more of that. No more!'

'You did do it once. I recall seven years ago at Flat Rock — '

'Seven years ago, D'Arcy — and that is the point exactly! I did it and I didn't like it and whoever thinks I'm going to shut down my ranch, leave it to the varmints and highbinders like Fenner, and ride off to a final moment of glory should just scrape off what's on the bottom of my boots and use that for brains.'

Cougar paused, then asked, 'Just who is the fool who sent you to find me?'

'Directly or indirectly?' D'Arcy asked, annoyed.

Carroll Cougar's green-gray cat eyes flashed with impatience and anger. Was he locked in with a madman after all? 'Either,' he managed to say, sawing his teeth together.

'General Plunkett caught up with me in Nacogdoches. I'd been . . . well, I was working up that way.'

'What in the world was Colonel Plunkett — did you say 'General' Plunkett? — well, I guess he would be by now. What was he doing up there?' Now Cougar's interest had been piqued if ever so slightly. Cougar and D'Arcy used to ride scout for the old man in Dakota Territory. A long way from Nacogdoches, Texas.

'Actually, he was looking for you, Cougar. He'd heard from somebody that I was in the area and he thought that if I didn't know where you were that maybe I could find you. I thought I could. There were a lot of nights we sat together around a fire with you talking about raising horses down this way some day, that it was good open country and all. Good graze, good water. I sort of volunteered to give it a try for the old man. It took a month and a half for me to find you, partner. Next time hide out nearer to civilization, will you?'

'What did Plunkett want?' Cougar's impatience had returned. D'Arcy could read that clearly in his eyes.

'Sorry,' D'Arcy apologized. 'I take the long way around the point sometimes. I've brought you a letter to read.' D'Arcy slipped two fingers inside the sweatband of his hat and pulled out a faded, folded letter. 'Look at the signature first. Then I'll tell you about it.'

With curiosity Cougar unfolded the letter and his eyes narrowed sharply. He looked at D'Arcy inquiringly as if suspecting some kind of a hoax. It wasn't every day that a man got a letter from President Ulysses S. Grant. He scanned the message and then placed the letter down with both hands.

'You see, Carroll,' D'Arcy said solemnly. 'It's no joke — it's critical.'

Cougar glanced at the letter again and the shock was such that it seemed to shrink and fold in his fingers. The name 'Grant', of course, meant something to everyone. The other name mentioned was uttered only by a few and meant nothing to any but those in a small, exclusive circle of men. Cougar was one of these.

Reineke.

'It's no joke at all, Carroll. Grant has asked for you personally.' D'Arcy's eyes lowered and narrowed. 'It's Reineke, all right. They want you to find him. Track him down and kill him.'

It was then that Cougar kicked the table over and let out a bellow that was savage, unexpected, and only barely human.

D'Arcy had managed to leap back as Cougar's boot came up. He sent his chair toppling to the floor in his scramble. The man D'Arcy faced now was frozen across the shoulders with the rigid, hunched tension of violent anger. Cougar's fists were bunched beside his thighs. His eyes could have taken slices out of plate steel.

'Tell me,' Cougar said hoarsely, and D'Arcy knew he had his man. The gamble had worked. He had ridden a long way to find Cougar and now the real man had come alive again. They had Cougar and that meant that all of them — from President Grant on down — might just have a small chance of winning the incredible and critical game that had to be played out.

Smiling, D'Arcy righted his chair, leaned forward with his elbows on his knees, and said, 'Listen, it's like this . . . '

2

Solon Reineke was the one who had murdered Carlina.

He had killed her in her bed while Cougar was out of the camp in the piñon pine-studded hills east of Defiance Mesa.

He had come and taken Carlina while she slept and killed her, leaving Cougar to come back and find her naked and crumpled and small against the cold earth.

That was the man D'Arcy was speaking of.

When he had met Carlina, it was the first time Cougar had first thought of settling down. He had ridden the ridges and the deserts too much before to find a woman of his own, the decent kind a man could rely on, who would settle and bear children for him.

What was a man to do? Ask a woman

to take up the wild ways and ride the long hills through the constant discomfort? No decent woman would wish to, and Cougar believed no decent man would ever ask a woman to deprive herself like that. What would they do, travois their babies along behind them, never having a doctor, never sure if the next day's hunt would bring in meat for their bellies?

And so, before Carlina Polk, Cougar had resigned himself to never having a lady of his own, only casual relationships at distant outposts with women who would forget him the next day, when the next man rode in; to sleeping now and then with an Indian woman, rising day after day to look at another bleak sunrise, staring at the cold and bitter skies at night.

'Cougar?' D'Arcy interrupted his dark thoughts.

'Yeah?' the big man grumbled.

'Leave it alone for now,' D'Arcy said. 'I know what you're thinking.'

'I know you do,' Cougar said roughly.

'You were there.'

'I was, sure. But, Cougar — you've got to quit thinking it was your fault. It wasn't.'

'The colonel gave us a simple escort job and instead of protecting her I let her get murdered . . . It was my fault, Calvin. Where in hell is Reineke?' Cougar demanded, and the eyes he turned on D'Arcy were quite savage.

'That's why I'm here, Carroll, remember? No one knows where he is. That's the job they want you to accept. Find Reineke and kill him if need be.'

Cougar shook his shaggy head slowly, heavily. 'What does the army — the government — Grant — any of them care now?'

'This isn't about Carlina,' D'Arcy answered. 'She's just one of the reasons they chose you to try to track him down. They know you've plenty of personal motivation.'

'Yes, I do. What is their reason for wanting him, Calvin?'

D'Arcy shook his head slightly. 'In a

while,' he said, willing to allow Cougar to ramble through his own dark thoughts for a time, sort himself out. He rose, his heavy chair scraping the wooden floor of the cabin. 'Why don't we go outside for now? I'll help you with that little job you have left to do. It's going to get hot out there; we can't leave them lying around in the sun. After we've finished that, we'll talk, all right?'

'All right,' Cougar murmured distantly, his own eyes lifting toward the open door. Together they went out into the clear light of the Texas morning and got to work along the riverbank where the soil was sandy.

D'Arcy watched Cougar. He had stripped off his shirt and the slabs of broad muscle moved in angry rhythm as he dug a grave for Trace Fenner. Sweat rolled off his powerful body. The two men did not speak. They simply worked and D'Arcy, studying Cougar, wondered if in the scout's mind he was digging another grave, in another place.

For another man . . . or for a small, delicate woman.

They spent little more than an hour at their work. When they were finished Cougar took both shovels and walked back to the tool shed, an open-shirted D'Arcy following.

D'Arcy paused to cool his head and torso at the water pump and when he went back to the cabin, drying himself as best he could with a kerchief, he heard Cougar clattering around inside the cabin, opening and closing drawers in the shallow corner cupboard.

'Looking for anything special?' the dark man asked as the scout tossed a few items on to the uprighted table and continued his search of the cupboard.

'No,' Cougar said without turning around. 'It's time to go, that's all. I'm collecting what I need.'

'I haven't told you yet what this is all about,' D'Arcy said as Cougar began making up a bedroll, throwing salt, sugar and coffee into a small canvas sack. 'There's more that needs explaining.'

'Explain it on the way,' Cougar said, grabbing his Winchester and placing it on the table beside the Spencer .56 he had brought back with him from the shed.

'I haven't even told you where we're riding!'

'Explain on the way,' Cougar said again, just as stiffly. He had made up his mind; they were riding.

Outside again, they crossed the yard to the pole corral where Cougar's horses watched him expectantly. The sun was hot on their backs, the grass sweet-smelling across the meadow. D'Arcy could hear the sounds of the pleasant creek wandering aimlessly through the cottonwood grove. Cougar unlimbered a rope and caught up a big, beautiful blue roan out of the small herd. He saddled in silence as D'Arcy stood with one foot on the bottom rail, watching him.

'Are we taking the other ponies with

us?' D'Arcy asked, nodding at Cougar's small, carefully picked remuda.

'Too much work. I'll be sending someone out from town to collect them,' Cougar replied, swinging into the saddle. 'There's a man named Joe Compton, runs the stable there, who's been wanting that sorrel and the paint. He'll take them all if I make him a price.'

'All right,' D'Arcy said tightening the cinches on his black horse's saddle. If Cougar's mind was made up, it was made up. He mounted as well and walked his horse up beside Cougar, who did not glance back at his prized horses as they started on their way, riding slowly across the yard before the little cabin. They dipped down into the cottonwoods, crossed the sun-sparkling stream, and rode out on to plains beyond.

The sky held clear. The horses moved easily across the long grass valley. Cougar spoke.

'Where is he, D'Arcy?'

'I told you, no one knows for sure.

The last time he was seen for certain he was near Alamogordo. We're guessing he's staying nearby. He knows a lot of people there. Anyway, for now that's our destination. Once we're in the area you can start to work. I did mention to General Plunkett that this was something like looking for a needle in a haystack, but he seems to think you're up to it. The instructions he gave me word for word were, 'You tell Cougar to find him — before Reineke starts a goddamn war!''

'Is that what Reineke's going to do?' Cougar asked almost indifferently. A cock pheasant rose unexpectedly nearly under his roan's hoofs and blurred away, drawing Cougar's gaze.

'Yes! If you'd let me talk, Cougar . . . ' D'Arcy said in frustration. Cougar was watching the pheasant go to ground again some distance off. The wind ruffled the long grass surrounding them, turning it silver.

'You'll have plenty of time to tell me on the way,' Cougar said starkly. He was interested in only one war — his own. It was fifteen minutes later before he spoke again to a now equally silent Calvin D'Arcy. 'Someone's following us, you know?'

D'Arcy nodded. 'Been following me since Nacogdoches,' the narrow man said. 'Want to stop and talk to them?'

'After we've taken care of business in town,' Cougar answered with an unconcerned shrug. 'Do you know who they are?'

'No. But I have a few guesses.'

'No matter,' Cougar said. 'After town we'll set up somewhere and ask them.'

They rode through a pretty little hollow with clumps of willow brush surrounding a small, stream-freshened pond and swung down there to water the horses. D'Arcy said, 'I noticed when you had your shirt off earlier . . . you still wear that necklace that Quiet Star made for you.'

'That's right,' Cougar said defensively. 'There's no reason behind it. Just habit.'

It wasn't really a necklace, only a hand-hammered and polished silver disc on a rawhide thong. Quiet Star had been young when she made it, very young. It was a childish attempt and there had been very little to work with in the way of tools on the reservation.

'She was a good kid,' D'Arcy said. He crouched down to sift the warm sand through his fingers. His horse's tail brushed his cheek and he swept it away.

'Good kid,' Cougar agreed gruffly and D'Arcy laughed.

'Is something funny, Calvin?' the big man demanded.

'No. Nothing, Cougar, nothing at all,' D'Arcy answered. 'It's just that sometimes you can make me laugh with the way you pretend that nothing matters to you at all.'

'Like what?' Cougar asked, scowling. 'Like a little Indian girl?'

'Like that,' Calvin D'Arcy said, deepening Cougar's scowl.

'Just a girl. She ran off of the

reservation. I took her back — she was squalling and scratching all the way. She ran off again and I took her back again.' Cougar frowned. 'The third time she got away.'

'And you couldn't track her?'

'The third time she got away,' Cougar said flatly. 'She had pluck, though, didn't she?' Now Cougar did grin. 'She stood up to General Crook himself that one time over the cornmeal being weevily.'

'I remember,' D'Arcy said. 'Crook's face all stony and red and you biting your tongue to keep from laughing.'

'It was that lousy sutler's fault . . . I always admired Crook, right from the start. Quiet Star just didn't understand that the man in command can't control everything that goes on in his outfit.'

'And you didn't bother to explain that to her!' D'Arcy laughed.

'I did . . . later,' Cougar said, still grinning. 'I didn't want to interrupt the show while she was at it.'

'Maybe,' D'Arcy said, breaking off

the figure he was tracing in the sand, 'we'll all be together again soon. Could happen, couldn't it?'

'I don't know what you're talking about. What do you mean?'

'General Crook is the one they want to kill — damn all, Cougar! If you'd let me get on with telling you the story . . . '

'After town,' Cougar repeated stubbornly. 'Besides, I don't like being here in the open while those men following us got the willows for cover.'

Then Cougar swung aboard the blue roan once more and D'Arcy shook his head and climbed into the saddle himself, muttering, 'Carroll Cougar, you are the most incurious and frustrating man I have ever encountered.'

But, whatever else he might be, Cougar was a fighter. Yes — Cougar was a hell of a fighter and D'Arcy was glad they were on the same side.

★ ★ ★

The town wasn't much to see. Cougar hadn't mentioned the name of it to D'Arcy, if it had one, and it didn't seem important enough to ask. A collection of shanties and low log buildings, a false-fronted hotel, and a deeply rutted main street with wagons drawn up in all directions and town dogs lazing wherever they felt like it. They rode directly to a dilapidated stable that still showed some of its ancient green paint on the side where the sun never struck it, and Cougar swung down to stride into its horse-scented depths to take care of his horse-selling business with the stableman, Joe Compton. D'Arcy squatted in the ribbon of shade beside the stable, holding his horse's reins as he let his eyes roam the town's streets and the surrounding countryside.

'They're here,' he said in a low voice when Cougar reappeared.

'I saw 'em from inside,' Cougar replied. Three men riding together, looking one way and the other, pausing hesitantly to ask a question. Not local men, then. They had moved out of sight now, but they were there. And obviously they did not care if they were seen or not, the way they conducted themselves.

'There were only three of them,' Cougar said. 'Back there I thought there were four riders.'

'There were. Like I say, they've been tailing me for a long way. There's four.'

Cougar nodded without comment. He had sold his horses for a fair if not grand price. That cut him off from the life he had had, the new life he had been trying to build for himself back along Twin Creek. The cabin would rot and give itself up to the elements and the critters. Only the land would remain. Maybe one day he would return to it, but for now he gave no thought to what he was trading away. Now there was only the job at hand to consider. Now he would listen to D'Arcy's tale.

They walked their horses slowly up the dusty, rutted street toward the restaurant and general store, which occupied most of a weed-covered corner lot. There was no sign of the riders who had been following them or their horses.

At a sign from Cougar, D'Arcy walked his black horse around to the back of the buildings as the scout tied up in front, his eyes taking in the length of the main street at a glance. A raggedy kid played in the street with a yellow dog and a red ball. Two cowboys lounged together in chairs placed in the shade of the awning at the hotel opposite. Two women in black hoisted their heavy skirts and crossed the street at a diagonal, laughing lowly. The rest of the town seemed to drowse behind closed doors. The men tracking them were not in evidence.

Cougar stepped up on to the sagging plankwalk in front of the store and strode across it to the badly hung red door. He eased inside and looked across the establishment to see D'Arcy at the rear near a stack of flour sacks. He shook his head and Cougar crossed to a table in the restaurant section of the building, seating himself. He placed the battered cavalry hat he was wearing on the floor near his foot, running a hand across his sandy hair as D'Arcy joined him and a tiny woman in blue gingham hurried toward the table.

'Hello, Mr Cougar,' she said in a mousy voice. He replied with a nod. 'We got everything pretty much the same as usual except that Buck brought in some antelope meat. We could cut you up a nice steak from it if you like?' She looked at the two men almost hopefully and Cougar nodded assent, guessing that the restaurant was running low on meat if Buck was having to go out hunting for it.

Across the way in the emporium section of the building, a woman browsed idly through bolts of cloth and an older man stood impatiently at the counter, a tin of tobacco in front of him.

'Where do you think our friends

went?' D'Arcy asked.

'Right on through town, I guess. Maybe to set up an ambush.' The waitress had returned with a huge pot of coffee, spilling some as she placed it down. When she had scurried away again to sell the old man his tobacco, Cougar said, 'Now, D'Arcy. Give me the whole of what's happening.'

3

'Do you recall John Dunn Hunter?' D'Arcy asked Cougar in a quiet voice.

Cougar nodded and filled his coffee cup.

'Sure I do. Most people thought he was crazy.'

'That could be,' D'Arcy said. 'I wouldn't know. I do know that he lived with the Indians for a time and came up with the idea of giving them a new homeland — even if it had to be taken by force of arms. He made himself a devil's bargain with Mexico.'

'That's right. He wanted to build an independent Indian nation between Mexico and the States. The idea suited Mexico fine. They have always worried about further incursions by the Americans.'

'Sure, but, Cougar, do you think Hunter was crazy, coming up with that idea?'

'I wouldn't know. It has some bent logic to it, I guess. Crazy? I don't know.'

'Do you think Solon Reineke is crazy?' D'Arcy asked, leaning further across the table to look directly into Cougar's eyes.

'I think he's a lousy, murderous bastard,' Cougar answered.

'Agreed. But this is what I mean: Reineke has the same idea as John Dunn Hunter had,' D'Arcy told him.

'What do you mean?'

'He wants the Apache, the Comanche, some of the Kiowas to set up a new empire, to reclaim what was once theirs.'

'Why would they listen to a white man's wild notion?' Cougar scoffed. 'Besides, it can't be done.'

'Probably not. It can get a lot of people killed, though.'

'It just can't be done. Even the angriest of the Indians are smart enough to know that. They'd be crazy to listen to such a wild scheme. They'll fight on in small bands for years to come, but this idea just can't work.'

'Couldn't it? What if Mexico agreed to help?' D'Arcy asked.

'They wouldn't. They've already learned their lesson. Why would they be willing to fight the United States now?'

'Maybe.' D'Arcy's voice dropped even lower. 'Then what if some European countries were willing to lend a hand, Cougar? Send money, men, arms?' Cougar's face took on a shadowed expression. D'Arcy persisted: 'Then would it be possible, if such an alliance could be constructed?'

'I don't see how . . . then again,' he shrugged, 'anything's possible, I guess. If you had enough men and equipment you could conquer the world, but realistically . . . ' He had another thought. 'Who else knows about this mad scheme, D'Arcy?'

'The president, his cabinet . . . us.'

'Why aren't they attempting a diplomatic solution?'

'I suppose they've tried, but look, no one is going to admit their government is involved, don't you see? This is supposed to look like a massive Indian uprising, not a land-grab by foreign powers.'

'Which is exactly what it is, of course.' Cougar sipped thoughtfully at his coffee. 'And of course that would be where Reineke's interests lie, not with the Indians' quest for self-rule.'

'Hardly,' D'Arcy said, his mouth forming a tight, humorless smile.

'You said something about General Crook.' The girl had arrived, served the food, and gone away. Cougar was no longer hungry.

'Yes. He's supposed to be killed. By white men. That is to be the sign of good faith to the Indians that their white allies are serious about the revolt. The Apaches, especially, hate Crook. He's whipped them in the past and pushed them farther and farther south into the Mexican Sierra Madres where they can barely survive. With him out of the way we've lost our most experienced and determined military man in the Southwest. We've got to protect him.'

'From Reineke.'

'From Reineke,' Calvin D'Arcy agreed. 'There's no doubt left that he's the mastermind behind the plan. Army intelligence had a man close to him at one time — missing now, of course — and it's Reineke. No doubt about it.'

'Damned traitor,' Cougar said. 'But why are we the ones who are supposed to protect Crook? Calvin, the man's got an entire army around him!'

'Yes, but suppose the assassin is someone Crook knows and trusts? Someone who once scouted for him, say? Remember, Cougar, Crook hasn't been alerted to this possibility yet. No one trusts the telegraph lines and besides, the general is more often found out in the field where there are no communications. We've got to reach him and then stop Reineke. Those are the orders. From the very top. As high as it gets.'

'Yes, you'd have to say that,' Cougar

said wryly. Jack Plunkett must have thought even more highly of his work than Carroll had thought to recommend him to the President of the United States for this mission. He could see, too, why Grant was so definite, why the orders had said not only find Reineke, but kill him. Orders of that sort weren't handed out frivolously.

On the surface Reineke's scheme seemed preposterous, but if the Indians were given all the weapons they needed, if there was an influx of money and equipment from Mexico, from Europe to attempt the destabilization of the young country, as D'Arcy had pointed out a lot of people would be killed no matter the end result. Possibly, he reflected quite soberly, as many as had been killed in all previous Indian wars together. If Reineke's mad grab for land proved impossible in the end, it would do the hundreds, the thousands in their graves no good.

'When is he going to try to

assassinate Crook?' Cougar wanted to know.

'No one knows. But a defector from his band has said it's definitely going to be soon. The Indians are sharpening their knives, waiting for the sign.'

'You're sure Crook doesn't know?' Cougar asked.

'He's bivouacking in the mountains, Cougar. He has no way of knowing about the death threat until we get there. We are the couriers. I've a message from the President for him, explaining pretty much what I've told you. If we're too late to stop General Crook's murder . . . well, then we'll find out if Reineke's whole damned scheme works, won't we?'

Cougar just shook his head. The idea was so incredible, terrible, but all too possible. As to the success of it — Cougar thought that success still seemed a small possibility, but it would not be the first time groups of men had decided to set up their own nations in the still unsettled West. Mexico would be glad for the chance to get back a chunk of the country. And the foreign powers — D'Arcy hadn't specified which were involved — had always been hungry for a piece of the continent, from the French to the Russians.

The little bell on the red door tinkled as Cougar ran through his thoughts. The man who entered made two mistakes. First, he thought Cougar hadn't seen him. Second, he was just too slow with his draw.

'Cougar!' D'Arcy yelled out in warning, but Cougar was already moving. He spun from the chair, went to one knee and fired as the man in the doorway loosed two quick, wild shots in Cougar's direction.

Cougar flinched as the two slugs impacted in the wall behind him, but his own aim had been steady. His Colt had been in his hand even before D'Arcy had called out, his finger twitching in response even as the man in the doorway fired his revolver at them.

His bullet slammed into the gunman's body and he was slapped around, banging into a stack of tinned goods. He clawed at the counter, which was smeared with his own blood even before Cougar's second shot and D'Arcy's first ripped through muscle and cartilage, finishing the deadly chore.

The gunman hit the floor and lay still as the last few cans from the pyramid beside him rolled down beside his body. Cougar lifted himself to his feet and walked to the dead man, his gun held loosely beside his thigh, D'Arcy at his heels.

'Do you recognize him?' D'Arcy asked as they stood over the fallen gunhand.

'Yeah. I know him. He's another one of the Fenner boys.' He reloaded his pistol and holstered it. 'Maybe it was time for me to clear out of this territory anyway.'

After helping the store owner and the ashen-faced little woman to clean up the place, buying a few provisions and apologizing again for the incident, the two men rode out westward. They rode warily, eyes alert and constantly moving across the oak-studded, long-grass country ahead of them. The tracking men were still out there somewhere, waiting.

'Do you have any idea who those four are?' Cougar asked D'Arcy. 'You said earlier that you had an idea.'

'General Plunkett told me that he thought it was known who they were,' D'Arcy answered. 'He wasn't positive, but the information he had indicated that they might be foreign-hired men. Prussians, to be specific.'

'They're in on this?' Cougar asked with surprise.

'So it seems. Of course, they could be strictly mercenaries. The Prussians have a long history of that, as you know.'

'I don't agree with Plunkett's informants, whoever they are,' Cougar said with a shake of his head. 'These gunnies are Western men. You can tell it by the way they sit their horses. 'No European looks like that in a saddle.'

'You could be right,' D'Arcy answered, glancing up as a passing cloud shadowed the land. 'They could be anyone. All sorts of men can be hired for a few American dollars . . . or for foreign gold.'

'I know it. And it worries me,' Cougar said. 'If these men — whoever they are — know who we are and where we're headed, why, then a lot of other people might have been warned. We could be running a gauntlet, D'Arcy. It could be there's a regular army of mercenaries out there.' Cougar squinted ahead toward the horizon where the hazy hills had begun to lift from the skyline at their approach.

'What do you suggest we do about it?'

'Do about it?' Cougar smiled thinly. 'I can't think of much we can do. We can only take one situation at a time.'

D'Arcy waited. He had known

Cougar for a long time. The big man with the faded cavalry hat and fringed buckskin shirt was hardly speaking aimlessly. He hadn't completed his thought and D'Arcy prodded him now.

'You're thinking about these men ahead of us,' D'Arcy said.

'Yes. They are the present situation, aren't they? What I intend to do it is this — we talk to them, D'Arcy. We ask them what they want and suggest they quit dogging our tracks.'

'And if they don't feel like talking?'

'Then,' Cougar said with a glance at his companion, 'they'll just have to feel like dying.'

'How were you intending to go about arranging this, Cougar?'

'They know where we're going. Or they think they do. They'll be lyin' ahead of us at some point with good cover.' His arm lifted and described an arc. 'We can ride off toward the north and pick up the line of the hills there. You can see good timber here and there and plenty of ridges and hollows. It's rougher ground, but it won't take us much longer to ride that way even if there's no trap set ahead of us. If there is an ambush arranged, our maneuver will flush them out of concealment. They'll have to come hightailing it after us or lose us in the rough country.'

'It should work if we get some altitude on them and find our own hiding place to watch the flats. Cougar — you haven't forgotten that there were four men; now there's only three. Meaning there's still one of them behind us somewhere?'

'If he wants to, he's welcome to follow along.'

Cougar smiled briefly, took his Spencer rifle from its boot, placed it across the saddlebow, and gradually swung the blue roan northward toward the convoluted hills.

It was a pretty stretch of country with grass and scattered oaks watered by the occasional, brilliantly flashing rills, which ran off the higher lands and wound their way southward, slowly dying as the thirsty land of the flats soaked up the water. There were scattered wildflowers, purple and white lupins and patches of yellow-flowered mustard. In the bottoms cottonwoods lifted their silver-green heads above the tangles of willow brush. A doe and her twin fawns took to their heels at the riders' approach.

Cougar saw all of this, though he was not looking at the land as a place of beauty, but as a battle map spread out before him, noting every hollow and river cut that might provide shelter, any ravine that might offer escape — or ambush.

He had trained himself long ago, in Dakota with George Crook, then a lieutenant with the 23rd Infantry, to see the land in that way. A warrior had no time to note the rising of a partridge from cover or the quick-winged blur of quail in flight except to see them as a possible sign of an enemy's approach. It was easy to fall into the habit of watching the long shadows spread in the twisted western canyons, touching the mesas with deep color, to sit spellbound by the long flow of the snowy mountains cut by tumbling white rivers — too easy to let the eye miss the smaller item which might mean death in the vast land.

D'Arcy commented on something that might become important. 'Looks like it could rain,' the thin man said. He lifted his chin toward the foothills.

Just above their ridged line it was possible to see a brooding strip of deep gray. Cougar just nodded. Even as he watched, a tendril of cloud slipped through a dark notch in the hills, snaking toward them. The wind had cooled and shifted to the north.

'Might,' he answered laconically.

And would that help them or aid their adversaries? There would be more concealment if the rain came in thickly, but Cougar wanted to spot the enemy first. He wasn't trying to run; he was trying to lure the pursuing band of men out into the open.

They let their horses graze for a time at an upland pond formed by one of the sparkling little rills spilling out of the foothills. Without appearing to, both men now continually conducted a visual search of the land behind them and the surrounding country, watching for a moving shadow, perhaps the quick glint of sunlight on metal, the startled flight of birds.

There was little doubt now that it would rain. Clouds in grotesque shapes lifted massive menacing heads above the hill, forming a mask against the sky, and the wind had increased and grown still colder. It gusted down the funneling canyons, flattening the grass.

By the time they had returned to their saddles they were able to see the slant of rain falling distantly. Still there was no sign of their pursuers. Maybe they had both been wrong in their assumptions.

Nevertheless they kept to their plan, riding toward, and then into, the time-scoured, cloud-darkened hills where the trails were forced to follow convoluted paths and the hollows were filled with concealing brush and stunted trees.

Now it did begin to rain. It was still a light rain, but the clouds darkened the land further yet. Cougar reached for his rain slicker and struggled into it as he rode, leaving it open in the front so that it flapped in the wind, giving him quicker access to his revolver. He still had his Spencer .56 handy, but if something popped up near at hand he wanted the Colt available.

'It's going to get a lot worse,' D'Arcy said, having to raise his voice a little against the whispered whine of the wind and the steadier slapping of the rain against their slickers. 'We might have to hole up for a while.'

'If it gets worse we will,' Cougar agreed. In fact he had come to the conclusion that the concealing rain suited his purposes just fine although they had to slow their progress as the clouds lowered even more.

It grew colder again, darker, the rain pelting down before a gusting wind now. Cougar gestured with his rifle toward a close stand of old oaks across the arroyo that now cut their trail, the rocks in its bottom gleaming coldly in the rain as a thread of a stream began to flow down its bottom.

Among the trees were large, broken boulders in a clustered, irregular monument. They were big enough to conceal men and horses. It was there that Cougar meant to halt.

'Make for them as soon as we dip out of the arroyo,' Cougar called above the rain rush to D'Arcy, who nodded his understanding.

Both horses slipped into the brush-clotted arroyo bottom and were sure-handedly guided by their riders' hands up and out, striking a course toward the wind-blustered oaks and the shelter they promised.

D'Arcy rode slowly into the cover of the trees, aware that the rocky ground underfoot was rugged enough that his horse would have to pick its way carefully over the slippery stones. He was also thinking that there was a possibility that their pursuers might have chosen this very spot to lay their ambush.

That wasn't the case, he realized with a sense of relief. Weaving his way into the copse, D'Arcy swung down heavily beneath a crooked, rustling oak and looked around him as Cougar himself approached and dismounted, standing there in the misting rain looking out at the long backtrail through the cottony gray of the low clouds. A scimitar of lightning slashed downward once and was followed almost immediately by the angry rumble of thunder.

'There's nobody back there,' D'Arcy said.

'Nobody I can make out, no.'

Cougar had slipped out of his rain slicker and he stood there still watching the backtrail with narrowed eyes, the wind whipping the fringes of his buckskin shirt.

'Go ahead and lead the horses up into that notch,' Cougar said, indicating a projecting boulder six or seven feet high with a squared top. The boulder, thirty feet long, had been split in two by eons of weather, a sort of platform having formed in the process. Twin oak trees stood protectively beside the boulder.

'All right,' D'Arcy agreed. It was shelter of sorts from the rampaging storm, and a good defensive position should anyone try to approach. 'Where are you going to be, Cougar?'

'Me?' Cougar said with some surprise, 'Why I thought you'd figure that, Calvin . . . I'm going hunting.'

'Better let me help you,' D'Arcy said, his brow furrowing with concern.

'You stay here and help yourself,' Cougar said. 'I'm going out afoot to see what I can find. If I can't do the job on my own I don't want you there trying to back me up. One of us, remember, has to get through to General Crook.'

D'Arcy started to argue, but he could

see Cougar's logic. Besides, you might as well talk to a tree as talk to Cougar when he got that look on his face. D'Arcy gathered the horses' reins and clambered up into the cleft. Looking back as he reached it, he had a last fleeting look at the receding back of the stalking man as he moved out from beneath the trees into the cold rain and the waiting battle.

4

It was what Cougar had been born to do. Time and experience had honed his natural hunting skills into deadly near-perfection, but he knew there was something in his blood, something he had been born with, an instinct that most men do not have. He had been born to wage war. It was not something he was proud of or boasted of, but he was well aware that the blood of warriors ran through his veins.

He eased down the arroyo a hundred yards from where they had crossed with the horses, half-sliding down across the slippery ground, rifle in hand, keeping well below the concealing wall of red earth as he reached the bottom and worked his way northward.

Cougar was a stalking creature now, alert only to his task. The rain plastered his shaggy hair across his face. His heart beat strongly but evenly. The steel of his rifle was cold in his hands — cold and comforting.

He couldn't see the rocks where D'Arcy had taken up his position from here, but he knew the dark man was up there and ready for any eventuality, his own sharp eyes searching the cloud-obscured field of battle. It was a comforting feeling. D'Arcy was a spectacular shot, perhaps better than Cougar himself. D'Arcy neither hesitated nor flinched. He shot to get the job done.

The soft rustling in the underbrush turned Cougar's head sharply, but it was only a grumbling boar breaking through the sumac and sage to escape the intruder on two legs.

Cougar crossed the arroyo bottom, which was beginning to run a fair amount of water, then climbed out up the red rock-face of it, and in a low crouch moved into the pinyon and live-oak woods beyond. His position now, above the trail he and D'Arcy had followed, was satisfactory, he decided, and he settled in for a while to catch his breath and peer more intently down the backtrail from his new viewpoint.

It was a brief, shadowy movement that he saw through the iron mesh of the rain; not enough to determine with certainty what it was, but enough to cause him to briefly stop his breath in feral anticipation.

Without realizing it he had drawn back the hammer on the Spencer carbine. Now he settled in, forcing himself to be utterly patient. His eyes seemed not to blink as he continued to study the spot at the verge of the woods where he had seen some sort of movement.

Then a horse nickered and he was sure. He smiled thinly and started toward the sound, moving with infinite care through the trees where the damp underfooting muffled his steps.

Once more lightning streaked the sky, again thunder spoke with a threatening voice, and Cougar, moving more swiftly now, worked his way downslope.

Time and again he paused, hoping for another sight, another sound of the enemy's movements, but all the world seemed shuttered by the downpouring rain, silenced by the muffling clouds.

Cougar crouched and waited among the trees. His buckskin shirt dripped water. It grew heavy on his back as the rain was absorbed. His jeans were just as sodden. He ran the back of his hand across his eyes, clearing the water from them. Then he heard his quarry speak. It was indistinct, still distant, but through the rain a portion of the words reached him clearly.

'They . . . probably rocks . . . '

Cougar's lips parted, showing his teeth in a dangerous smile that would have warned the enemy of his intent if they could have seen it. But first he had vowed to talk to them — or try to. There was, after all, a chance that he and D'Arcy could be wrong in their judgment, that these were not the stalking men they were concerned about. Not hired killers but innocent travelers. But those who go trailing others with guns through this kind of weather were very unlikely to have a good end in mind.

Cougar again worked his way carefully downslope. Clouds smothered the hilltop now, seeming to swirl past his feet as he slipped toward his adversary. He found he had grown even more cautious now, more patient since he had located them. There was no hurry at all.

The first man stepped suddenly from behind the trunk of a towering, wind-shuffled oak tree and fired nearly point blank at Cougar, but the man's boots had made a brief, whispery noise against the damp leaves as he moved, and the ratcheting click of the hammer on his rifle had been too loud in the vast silence. Cougar, alerted, threw himself to the leaf-littered ground beneath him, rolled, and fired as he came to his feet again.

The gunman's bullet had whipped past Cougar, ripping shreds of bark from a fallen pine. He was young, Cougar saw in that brief instant. His eyes, set above prominent cheekbones, were savage, nearly black, his expression triumphant.

His triumph lasted a single heartbeat more.

Cougar's Spencer's muzzle dusted sparks against the fog as the bullet flew true to its mark and the ambusher flew backward, the round from the large-caliber rifle tearing its twisting way through jacket, heart, and spine.

For a moment the kid gunman stood leaning against a tree as if nailed there by the slug. Then he slid slowly down. The rifle he carried dropped from his hand to the dark, sodden earth. Now he lifted his empty hand and a finger pointed at Cougar in a gesture meaningful only to the gods of death and pain.

He sat against the earth, legs spread, and was silent.

Cougar's eyes flashed as he moved to the tree himself, using its cover against any onrushing attackers, but there were no more shots, no footsteps of men approaching on the run. Carefully, he crouched and patted the man's pockets, coming up with a chamois purse of some weight that had been tucked into the gunman's belt.

Curious, Cougar had started to open the purse when he heard the thunder of guns from across the arroyo.

'Dammit!' *They had gone after D'Arcy.*

Cougar headed back toward the rockpile at a scrambling run. He slipped and went to one knee as his boot struck an unseen tree root. Still the shots rang out across the arroyo. He could see darker smoke rising through the low clouds. They continued to ring out. Six, ten — too many to continue counting. Cougar reached the arroyo at a run and half-slid, half-fell down to its rocky bottom, clambering up the far side frantically, the fingers of his free hand clawing at the mud, tearing themselves on rock.

Reaching the crest he forced himself to slow: it wouldn't do to charge headlong into the bullets. They rang out occasionally still and then stopped abruptly, only a few lingering echoes drifting on the wind through the rain. That could be good . . . or it could be a terrible sign.

It was terrible.

Easing through the trees, rifle at the ready, his chest rising and falling with exertion, hair washed into his eyes, Cougar came upon the site of the massacre.

Both horses were down, dead. The blue roan looked up at him with black, stony eyes. The black horse of D'Arcy had been riddled with bullets.

'Cougar . . . ' The voice was only a rasping whisper. Cougar recognized it, though, and he moved toward its source.

D'Arcy was among the rocks, propped up to allow him to fire back at his attackers. One arm hung uselessly at his side and there was blood on his shirt front even with the constant rain washing it away.

'Where are they?' Cougar asked, crouching beside his friend.

'Gone . . . think they went looking for you. Don't know . . . ' D'Arcy's voice trailed off weakly.

Looking around the notch carefully first, Cougar placed his rifle aside and opened D'Arcy's shirt. The wound in his chest was more bloody than serious, it seemed. A flap of flesh showed where a bullet had glancingly struck rib bone and exited. It was probably a ricochet, he estimated.

The one in the upper arm had been a solid hit. Cutting away the sleeve of D'Arcy's shirt Cougar found a jagged, furrowed wound slashed across D'Arcy's shoulder.

'Can you move it?' Cougar asked.

'Maybe. I don't want to try,' D'Arcy answered with a sickly grin.

'All right. Try to stay alert and keep

watch for me. 'I've some bandaging in my saddle-bags.'

'Sure,' D'Arcy grunted. Already his eyes were closing of their own accord, the lids drawing down as if by unseen weights. He fought against the closing curtains. He was deathly pale and now he began to tremble as shock set in. Cougar put a hand briefly on his friend's arm and scuttled toward his dead horse.

He yanked the saddle-bags from beneath the stiffening blue roan and moved back to where D'Arcy sat dismally in the rain, teeth chattering, his eyes only slits.

'We'll patch you up,' Cougar said gently.

'Yeah . . . all we need's a new arm to screw on,' D'Arcy answered, trying for a humorous note and a smile that just didn't work. Cougar smiled back and set to it, doing what he could with what he had to work with, which wasn't a whole lot.

D'Arcy passed out before Cougar

had finished with the wound in his side, splashing it with carbolic and stitching it up clumsily with gut.

For the arm he could do little more. The bone wasn't broken, but the muscles themselves were peeled back. The bullet had mushroomed on impact and torn tendons and meat to shreds. Maybe a surgeon could have repaired them, but Cougar was no surgeon. There was nothing he could do but apply the disinfectant and bind arm and shoulder up as tightly as possible. Already Cougar knew that Calvin D'Arcy's arm would never be of much use to him again, and only time would tell if it was going to have to be removed. Cougar's unhappy guess was that it would be a job for a sawbones.

'Now what?' he asked himself as he finished his grisly work and sat back on his heels, hat tipped back, studying D'Arcy and the aftermath of the ambush.

His enemies were still out there waiting for another propitious moment to finish their deadly task. Probably, as D'Arcy had guessed, they had circled back looking for Cougar after hearing the shots below, leaving D'Arcy for dead. By now they would have found their own dead accomplice and might be on their way back to finish the job. Or, he considered, they could be waiting, holding their position in the rain, just watching — after all, they now knew where Cougar was.

Thinking about the man he had killed, Cougar took the chamois purse he had taken from the body and opened it. There were only a few items in it: a tooth from an adult, a molar; some gold money; six new-minted double eagles; a couple of foreign-minted gold pieces; and a note written in a language Cougar didn't comprehend but assumed to be German.

He put these items back in the purse, pocketed it, and made his decision without wasting more time on consideration. General Crook himself, who had learned his own frontier warfare tactics from the Indians, had promulgated the theory of constant movement, never allowing oneself to be pinned in a known position. Cougar's position was known — therefore he must move no matter the dangers and difficulties involved.

Cougar squatted down, hoisted D'Arcy in a fireman's lift, and started off beneath the weight of his wounded friend into the rain and confusion of the night. Moving through the deepest brush he could find, he wended his way westward through the fits of the drenching storm. He slogged his way upslope over long ridges rife with pinyon and blue spruce, down and up canyons where freshets flowed, taking every trail a horse could not easily follow.

It was a heartbreaking march. The legs grew leaden, the muscles stiff and swollen, the mind blurred. It was enough to break a man, a forced march with a hundred and sixty pounds on his back, but then, Cougar was not an ordinary man. He was born with great size and a massive heart.

At fourteen he had killed a man quite by accident. He was as big as most full-grown men already at that age, stronger than most from chopping the wood, cutting hay, and moving stone to care for the family's poor Ohio farm. His father had gone off to the War and never returned with the rest of the Ohio Volunteers. Cougar came early to manhood.

The army officer who had insulted his girl cousin and tried to grab her from the seat of the buckboard couldn't have counted on a raw-boned kid menacing him. But Cougar, who had been raised on duty, toughened by his arduous young life, taught by his father to be always unafraid, had protected the girl in the only way he knew — with bare hands clenched into fists like granite blocks, impelled by shoulders like those of a blacksmith — and the officer had fallen dead in the mud of the Troy, Ohio street.

Cougar had fled in the middle of the night, his mother having packed him a small get-along bag of provisions, handing him his father's old Hawkens rifle, kissing him drily.

'You were a man today,' the old woman had said as her small, dry hands held his thick, meaty-knuckled ones. 'Go and make your way as one now.' Then she had turned and walked inside the cabin, closed the door and drawn the latchstring and Cougar was left alone in the world.

He had worked his way West as a wagoneer's swamper, growing stronger and world-wiser yet. After the teamster had broken an axle on his rig at Fort Ransom, Dakota Territory two years later, Cougar, already tired of his trade, volunteered for the army. He was just sixteen, but no one had questioned the age of this tall, broad, self-confident young man with the sandy hair and strange, gray-green eyes. The Sioux and the Cheyenne were talking war and the army was accepting all capable volunteers.

Cougar was more than capable. He fought as an enlisted man for two years before, tiring of less-than-adequate officers and NCOs, he put himself forward as a scout and, under the tutelage of an old canny man named Spanner and a young Osage Indian called Cornhawk, became one of the best trackers on the far plains.

Cougar had seen war in Dakota and Wyoming, in Apache country along the border, and on the broad plains with the Cheyenne and Lakota Sioux. He had lived through the smoke and fires of hell before he was twenty-one.

He was no longer so young, but he hoped he had grown wiser. What lay ahead of him now would take all that he had learned in the years gone past. And if he did fail this time it would not be a battle that would be lost, but a war.

5

The manzanita was thick, the sage heavy with water. The night was coming in. A crimson bow seemed to be arched above the last misted yellow ball of the sun on the western horizon. The storm clouds, finished with their mischief, were breaking up, speeding away on the cold winds. The man in the buckskin shirt trudged on across broken hillsides, his burden weighing heavily across his broad shoulders.

Cougar couldn't count the number of times he had slipped and fallen that day, bringing a groan from the lips of Calvin D'Arcy, how many times he had paused for breath as his lungs ached savagely, how often he had stopped to look uncertainly along the backtrail for his pursuers. He only knew that the day had seemed endless, the miles covered few, and with each mile he was forced to travel in this plodding fashion, the nearer he was to failing in his mission. He would arrive too late, if not at all.

General Crook was hundreds of miles away and he was afoot on bad country with a badly wounded man. They would never be able to stop Reineke, never be on time to head off the coming disaster. Once, during a brief, rain-soaked rest, D'Arcy had lifted his hand and said with what seemed to be the last of his breath, 'Just get out of here, Cougar! Damn you, leave me here.'

Cougar had given him no answer but a stubborn shake of his head, and after a few minutes more he had again hoisted his friend and slogged on through the rain, into the wilderness and the coming darkness of falling night.

Now, stumbling across the broken, treacherous ground of the hillslope, he was forced to admit to himself that he was going to have to work his way down to the flats into more open country if he was to have any chance of finding some sort of settlement, any sort of habitation before D'Arcy perished. Cougar scoured the country beyond and below him again. It was a gray and folded land beneath the breaking cloud cover. Nothing moved but the wind-drifted clouds themselves. He and D'Arcy had not talked about it, but both knew they were well into Comanche country now. They had trusted to their horses, much larger and stronger than Indian ponies, and to their weapons to keep them from danger. Now, afoot, there would be no escape at all if the Indians came hunting.

A few miles back Cougar had seen the remnants of an ill-plotted railroad spur and an ill-conceived town on the plains: twin rusted rails ending abruptly at a pile of ashes and burned timbers. The Comanches had spoken clearly: 'No farther.'

Cougar swayed a little as he hefted his burden and started on again under shadowed skies. D'Arcy still lived;

Cougar could feel the involuntary movements of his body from time to time, a hand that occasionally clenched Cougar's shoulder in thanks or in silent plea. D'Arcy was alive, but for how much longer? How much could a man endure?

Cougar found a narrow, grassless canyon and started down it, aiming once again for the flatlands. The sunset had diminished to a purple glow above the canyon rim. The wind, not abating with the cessation of the rain, nudged at his back as he worked carefully along the rocky canyon floor.

He rounded a bend in the canyon walls and stopped dead.

The fire was small but it glowed plainly in a hollow cut into the dark canyon wall, splashing the bluff behind it dimly with moving light and shadows. Cougar drew back into the darkness and stood motionlessly in the thickness of gathering night, remaining absolutely still, watching. D'Arcy moaned softly and Cougar eased him to the cold ground where he lay without move-ment.

Then, with his rifle in his hands, the hammer drawn back, Cougar crept downward.

There were only two possibilities that he could think of: it was those men who had been hunting himself and D'Arcy, or it was a Comanche hunting party. No one else would be traveling this godforsaken, war-bound section of country.

Cougar was a silent, wary creature of the dark, drawn inexorably toward the faintly flickering fire; a night creature both repulsed and fascinated by its heat and light.

He paused to listen, to look up and down the canyon, away from the fire, but he saw nothing and heard nothing. There was only the overpowering scent of damp sage burning, the distant bark of a coyote, and the hushed sound of rain-heavy sand sloughing from the damp, dark walls of the long canyon.

Cougar debated, and then, deciding

there was no choice if D'Arcy were to survive, he moved nearer yet to the fire. If they were his enemies he meant to see them first, for as old man Spanner had once told him, 'The last one to know is the first one to go.' Cougar meant to know.

What he discovered was so far from what he had expected that it was at first startling, then, in an inexplicable way, angering.

The white man stood near the smoky fire, clearly silhouetted before the canvas top of the covered wagon that rested at some distance behind him. The man sipped coffee and glowered down at the low fire, muttering indistinctly once in a while. He wore a white shirt, black trousers, a black vest. The shirt was open at the neck, but Cougar suspected by its cut that it usually supported a cellophane collar and black tie. The man was small, unusually deep in the chest, but not healthily so, giving a pigeon image to his physique. His hair was dark, thin, slicked back carefully. He was clean-shaven and used many nervous motions of his free hand to accentuate whatever it was that he was muttering.

If the sight of this man in the wilderness was startling, what Cougar saw next was incredible. A woman came from around the wagon, her dark hair pulled back neatly into some sort of knot, her body trim and high-breasted. She wore a white blouse with a black velvet choker around her slender neck and a divided black riding skirt brushing the tops of her boots as she walked.

The man saw Cougar first as he emerged from the shadows into the ring of firelight and he dropped his cup, his eyes goggling as he stuttered: 'Who are you?' He dropped back an involuntary step at the sight of the wide-shouldered intruder in his camp.

'Carroll Cougar, and what manner of fool might you be?' Cougar responded roughly.

''*Fool*'?' It was the girl who replied

sharply. 'How dare you call my father a fool — whoever you are.'

Cougar answered evenly, 'I call any man a fool who's out wandering in this country, drawing a wagon, leading a girl, building a fire the size of a barn for the Comanches to see.'

The man ignored all of Cougar's speech and replied in a quavering voice, 'I am Dr Morris White. This is my daughter, Ellen. If yours is the Western manner of hospitality, God save the South.'

'What sort of doctor might you be?' Cougar asked hopefully.

'I am a doctor of medicine, sir,' White responded, puffing up a little now, steadying his voice. 'And may I say, sir — '

'There is such a thing as luck in this world, then,' Cougar interrupted. 'I've a badly injured man with me. I'll bring him in. Grab your bag, sir. You, girl,' he commanded, 'prepare him a bed.'

The girl's mouth opened in astonishment and anger, but she had no chance to answer as Cougar spun on his heel and slipped out again into the darkness, returning with D'Arcy slung heavily across his shoulder.

'What's wrong with him?' the doctor asked before Cougar had placed his friend on the hastily made bed the girl had spread on the ground near the fire.

'Gunshots. I'll have coffee — you see to him,' Cougar said peremptorily. Again the girl opened her mouth to reply, but her father called to her before she could speak. Cougar only heard her mutter the word 'rude' as she turned to fetch her father's medical bag from the wagon. Cougar poured himself a cup of coffee and hunched down near the warm glow of the fire, his buckskin shirt steaming with the heat. He tossed a few more sticks of brush on to it and frowned. Let the girl think what she wanted. All he cared about was seeing that D'Arcy was tended to. The opinion of that little slip of a girl mattered nothing to him.

The doctor unwrapped the bandages

Cougar had so hastily bound D'Arcy's wounds with and the rudimentary stitches he had administered and said to Cougar, 'You've butchered him.'

'There wasn't a whole lot to work with, nor time to do it better,' Cougar growled back.

Muttering under his breath, the doctor got to work, occasionally asking his daughter for something. Cougar didn't watch them at their work, nor did he watch the fire. He looked constantly up their backtrail, knowing he still had enemies out there, not knowing if they had managed to cut his sign. In the darkness and rain he thought not, but if they spotted this fire they would be certain to come calling.

He did not feel that he had put these two in danger by coming here. They had put themselves into it. Waddling across Indian country in a wagon with no one to fight for them but themselves, which they seemed ill-equipped to do, was nearly criminal in its stupidity. Cougar felt only grateful that Fate, which had played him so many dirty tricks in his time on this earth, had this once condescended to place help for D'Arcy across his path. His friend was a good one and he would certainly have died on the trail the way things were going. Cougar had long tired of burying good friends in desolate, unmarked graves.

It was nearly an hour later when the doctor, dabbing at his forehead with a folded handkerchief, sleeves rolled back, approached Cougar and told him, 'He hasn't got a real good chance. Gangrene is apt to set into that arm. It's badly shattered.'

'You've done what you could, I expect,' Cougar answered.

'We'll need some assistance lifting him up into the wagon,' the doctor said sourly. Obviously, he had taken no immediate liking to Cougar's brusque manner. Neither could that be helped, Cougar reflected. This was not the time or situation for niceties. Let the two of them think what they liked about him.

'Sure.' Cougar rose and ambled toward the wagon. The girl was inside, making a more suitable bed for the wounded man. When she was finished, Cougar's eyes on her, she spoke deliberately past the scout's shoulder to her father.

'It's ready now.'

Cougar went to where D'Arcy lay and scooped him up in his massive arms, bringing a small groan from the pale lips of his friend. Cougar walked to the wagon, sat on the tailgate, shifted his weight, and turned, lifting D'Arcy toward the bed. They settled him in, the girl covering him finally with a down coverlet.

That done, Cougar returned to the fire. The doctor appeared from the shadows, moving gingerly on his thin legs as if it pained him to walk at all, cradling an armful of dry brush for the fire.

'Leave that wood there,' Cougar said, 'that fire's big enough as it is.'

'Just who do you think you are?' the

girl, Ellen, demanded. 'Who are you to tell us what to do in our own camp?'

'A man who's seen too many Comanches,' Cougar replied, his eyes fixed on hers. 'There's no point in lighting a beacon for them. They'll find us soon enough as it is.'

The doctor stood indecisively for a moment, then dropped the armful of wood he held and turned and walked away, looking to his daughter as if for forgiveness. The girl watched him go. She herself removed a nearly empty lard can from the rear of the wagon and carried it nearer the fire where she plonked it down and sat next to where Cougar crouched, coffee cup in hand. She remained saucy despite her evident weariness.

'You think you're the lion returned to his lair, don't you?' she asked in a brittle voice. Her eyes were fire-bright and angry.

'In a way,' Cougar said expressionlessly. 'Wherever I live, that's my lair. Those who are there live my way.'

'And if they don't follow your arrogant rules?'

'Some don't,' Cougar said. 'Some of those have been known to die out of sheer spite when if they'd only listened to me they might have lived.'

'Because you are so brilliant,' she said mockingly.

'Because *they* weren't,' Cougar replied with a shrug. 'If you don't know where you're walking it's a good idea to listen to someone who's been there before.'

She sat sullenly, defiance bright in her eyes, watching the fire as it burned low and a few fitful sparks flew. Cougar might have been a stone beside her. He had resigned himself to the situation when she unexpectedly spoke.

'Where do you come from? Who are you?'

He laughed. 'How much time do you have?'

'Don't make fun of me. I don't like it.' She tucked her skirt more deeply between her knees. She still looked away from him. By the firelight

Cougar was struck by the beauty of her challenging eyes, the slope of her cheek, and attractive, defiant tilt of her chin.

'I wasn't making fun of you, lady,' Cougar said sincerely. 'It's just that I've traveled so many roads that I can hardly remember most of them. There's some I don't care to recall, too. As for asking me who I am — I haven't got an idea. I'm like most men. Folks define me as this or that and that's the way they see me forevermore. I don't have the time to spare to convince them of one thing or the other — I don't even take the time to define myself.' Again he made a small shrug, 'What's the point in all of that anyway?'

'I see . . . you don't want to tell me. You're probably some sort of outlaw or something,' she said, her voice dropping lower.

'No, miss,' Cougar said, finishing his coffee. 'It's just as I said — there's not much point in trying to explain what I am. I'm not sure I know. Just another vagabond roaming this earth, I suppose. That's my best explanation. What about you?'

'My father was chosen to accept a position with the government,' she said. 'He felt he was stagnating in St Louis. His practice, to be honest, was not flourishing, nor was the church.'

'What church?' Cougar asked.

'Father is also a doctor of theology,' she informed him with evident pride. 'Unfortunately St Louis is a stiff-necked town, not progressive enough to accept some of Father's tenets.'

'Ah, I see,' Cougar answered. The girl's mouth tightened at his manner. Cougar felt himself growing terribly weary; still, he was fascinated by this young, apparently courageous if foolish young woman, who had followed her father out onto the menacing plains and he wanted to sit with her, to speak to her. His response, he could tell, had not been appropriate. He had a knack for that. Her manner had stiffened again.

'You see what?' she inquired tightly.

'Your father. A minister, preaching things people didn't want to accept . . . isn't that what you said?'

'They didn't *understand*,' she said emphatically.

'A lot of people have a lot of different ideas about religion, miss. Anyway. You're saying they didn't like or understand whatever it was he was preaching. They quit bringing their problems to him and his church kinda floundered. Is that it, more or less?'

'They were narrow-minded bigots!'

'I wouldn't know. I don't spend much time thinking about that sort of thing. Maybe they were bigots. If you say so, I'll accept that. Anyway, the whole mess sort of finished off your father's preaching career and his medical practice as well, right?'

'Something like that,' she admitted with a deep sigh as if Cougar was incapable of understanding the matter even if she spent hours explaining it.

'What kind of government job has he landed?' Cougar asked, seeking to sidetrack the other conversation, which was obviously upsetting the girl. At his question she brightened a little. Ellen was obviously more optimistic about the future.

'Army surgeon,' she said proudly. 'He'll be working with General George Crook himself! I assume you've heard of *him*.'

Cougar reached for an answer but found himself unable to respond. Silently, he stared at the dying embers for a long minute. Then once again he shifted his eyes to the girl's face made bright and hopeful by the dull firelight and by pride in her father. 'Yes,' he answered simply, 'I've heard of him.'

'Ellen!' Dr White called out. 'It's time we were turning in. Dawn comes early.'

'Yes, Father.' She rose, started away, and then hesitated. She said nothing else. But she offered Cougar what was very nearly a smile, and then, hurrying away, she left him alone by the fire bemused and a little stunned.

Fate, he figured, had given him a

hand by placing Dr White across his path when D'Arcy needed medical help so badly. But there was always, it seemed, a twist to Fate that a man couldn't foresee.

White was Crook's new regimental surgeon, was he? That meant these two and their wagon were traveling in the same direction he was. So what now? There seemed only one option with D'Arcy down and injured as he was: he would have to travel on with them. He and D'Arcy no longer had horses even if Calvin had been capable of riding. It was urgent that he reach Crook and warn him of this plot of Reineke's to assassinate him.

It was important that he find Reineke and repay him for the rape and murder of Carlina Polk all those years ago.

And it seemed there was only one way to continue his search for Crook now, he thought, looking at the doctor's wagon where Ellen had disappeared. The only thing was, he was bringing a lot of trouble with him and he did not wish it upon this naïve pair. Then again, they unknowingly carried even greater troubles with them, traveling foolishly as they were into Indian country, a preacher and a tiny woman.

That was the way it was going to have to be, Cougar decided. In the morning he would talk to White and try to convince him what he was up against alone. In the meantime he sat and watched the fire burn down to coals as he listened to the night sounds, knowing that the killing men were still out there; not knowing when they would come again, but only that they would.

6

D'Arcy was awake and alert. Cougar sat on the wagon's tailgate talking to him as the land, red earth and silver-blue with sage, ran past beneath the wheels. It had taken a while for D'Arcy to orient himself and figure what had happened, but now he had a handle on things.

'Thanks, Cougar,' he said for the third time.

'Shut up,' Cougar growled.

'Not many men could have carried me out of there — fewer would have bothered to try.'

'Nice morning, isn't it?' Cougar said, peering out at the broad land from beneath the brim of that battered cavalry hat. 'Nice and fresh after the rain.'

'All right,' D'Arcy said, laughing. 'I give up!'

'You'd have done the same for me,' was Cougar's last comment on the episode. He knew that D'Arcy was trying to sincerely express his gratitude, but it was embarrassing in a way — a man doesn't need to be thanked for doing his duty. He sat silently then, seeing how deeply the wagon wheels cut their ruts into the red earth. It would not take long for a decent tracker to deduce what had happened to his quarry, chase the wagon down.

'There ain't all that many of them,' D'Arcy said, knowing his friend's thoughts. 'It would take a lot of nerve for them to come riding up on us while we still got teeth. Their ambush attempt was one thing — but they played that hand and lost a few cards.'

'Men are easy to come by, D'Arcy. Find me a town and a saloon, give me some Prussian gold, and I could raise an army.'

'It would take time, Cougar.'

'Not all that much. They'll be coming on. They have to stop us.' Cougar fell into an ominous silence. He removed his hat, placing it on the wagon bed beside his leg. The wind lifted his sandy hair from his scalp. He told D'Arcy soberly, 'They'll have to kill the doctor and the girl, too.'

'Why? They don't know anything,' D'Arcy said, sitting up so sharply that he winced with pain. He grabbed his side and lay back again on the soft bed Ellen White had made up for him.

'They have no way of knowing that,' Cougar reminded him. 'They don't know what we've told White and his daughter. They can't chance it, can't let this wagon get through to Crook.'

'You're right, of course,' D'Arcy said, glancing toward the front of the wagon. Through a gap in the Whites' stacked goods and the canvas beyond, he could just make out the backs of the two figures on the wagon's bench seat. 'If we don't win, they lose. Maybe we shouldn't have dragged them into this.'

'You'd be dead by now, D'Arcy, and

I'd be afoot if we hadn't done things this way.'

'I know,' D'Arcy sighed. 'It's just a damned shame to put them in peril. What also bothers me, Cougar, is trying to find Crook if he's still in the field. You know the general — he doesn't let anyone know where he is if he can help it.'

'I know,' Cougar replied. That went back to the time at Fort Apache when the 'blanket Indians' had set up a fairly elaborate intelligence network designed to alert Cochise and the other Indian leaders to the whereabouts of Crook's forces. It took little for these 'tame' Indians at the post to learn of Crook's intentions by listening to the soldiers' conversations and then pass the information on to the hostiles.

The Apaches were deadly enough, ghostlike fighters on their own; with knowledge of General Crook's movements they became, for a while, undefeatable.

'Still,' Cougar reminded D'Arcy, 'you

can't hide an entire army. You shouldn't have that much trouble finding him.'

'*Me?*'

'With luck you'll be fit enough to do it by then.'

'And just what did you plan on doing, Cougar?'

'I'm going to find Reineke. I'm going to tackle this problem from the other end. That gives us two chances to break this conspiracy up instead of the one we have if we stick together.'

'And,' D'Arcy said, knowing it for the truth, 'you want the man.'

'I want the man,' Cougar affirmed. He was silent again then, picturing in his mind the dark-eyed girl he had loved so. The flash of Carlina's smile, the curve of her breasts and hips, the long-legged stride, the glow in her eyes when she made love to him . . . and that damned Reineke had killed her, erased a beautiful vibrancy from the face of the earth. Under Cougar's nose, while she was under his protection. Reineke was to blame. Cougar was to blame as well, and he had been paying the price in guilt for a long while. Now it was Reineke's turn to pay. And he would pay with his blood.

Logically, Cougar knew that he should not entirely blame himself. There were five other men in the camp that night. Who would have thought Reineke callous enough to assault the woman there? But he had, and then he had shot her dead. His gun was still warm when Cougar rode into camp and the woman, blood smeared across her beautiful, pale breast, was already growing cold . . .

'Cougar,' D'Arcy said gently, 'come out of it. It's no good dwelling on it.'

'No,' Cougar agreed. 'It's no good.' But knowing that wouldn't keep the thoughts from constantly returning.

A voice from the front of the wagon, Dr White's, broke in on his bleak thoughts. 'There's a dwelling up ahead! A ranch, possibly even a small town. I can't tell yet.'

Cougar took a grip on the side board

of the wagon and swung out to peer ahead into the sunlight. He could make out a green stain against the red earth — grass — and two rooflines. There was a glint of reflection off of a small creek that flowed through a stand of cottonwoods and spread out to water the grass along its route. Now, too, he could see the dark figures of grazing cattle.

'What have we got, Cougar?' D'Arcy asked when the scout had swung around to resume his former position.

'A ranch, it seems. Possibly a stagecoach way station. A place where we can water the horses, anyway; maybe a chance for me to buy a couple of horses for us.'

D'Arcy laughed. 'What is it, Cougar? Are you getting antsy riding in a wagon?'

'Yes, aren't you?'

'Sure, but I've got no choice. For now I'm just going to try to relax and enjoy it.'

D'Arcy knew that it was not only the

lack of freedom that was chafing Cougar. If they were going to have a chance against the enemy, who was certainly still trailing them, it was necessary for Carroll Cougar to be mobile, to scout and be free to attack if necessary. A wagon was a target, nothing more. A man on horseback — if he was Carroll Cougar — could be counted as cavalry.

The town, if it could be called that, had no name. As Cougar had guessed it was a former way station for Butterfield Stage.

* * *

Before, they had had to give up that stretch of their line because of the new Indian hostilities.

Now it was poor, forlorn: a weathered, red wooden building with three adobe outbuildings flanking it. A narrow, muddy stream made its sluggish way through some scraggly cottonwoods. They drew their wagon

100

up in front of the main building where a buckskin horse stood dismally at the rail, patiently waiting for its owner. A dog started yapping in the distance and was called in.

Cougar slipped from the bed of the wagon and stood stretching his trail-weary muscles. D'Arcy looked at him enviously. He could probably have made it to his feet, but he was just in too much pain to make the effort for the time being.

'I don't suppose by some miracle they've got a beer in this godforsaken place,' D'Arcy said hopefully.

'I'll find out,' Cougar promised.

Dr White said, 'I hardly think that would be proper around a young lady.' Both men ignored the doctor's words.

'Just see if they've got any, will you, Cougar?' D'Arcy pled. 'I'm dry all the way down to my toes.'

'Not if you wish to continue to ride in my wagon,' Dr White said more sharply. He glowered at Cougar and D'Arcy for a moment, wanting to say more. In the end he just turned and walked stiffly away.

'No wonder they ran him out of St Louis,' D'Arcy said in wonder.

'It must have been some church,' Cougar agreed. 'No matter — I'll see what they've got to drink and ask around about getting us some horses.'

The interior of the building was low-ceilinged, dusty, and empty as Cougar entered it from the brilliant outdoor sunlight. He spotted a cider barrel and ambled that way, thinking that it might have to do to assuage D'Arcy's thirst. A little man with an egg-shaped head who looked as if he were surprised to find himself there wandered in from a back room, wiping flour-dusted hands on his bib overalls.

'Help you?' he asked Cougar. His pale, watery eyes blinked rapidly as he spoke.

'The main thing I wanted was to ask if you might know of any horses around that might be for sale,' Cougar replied. 'There was that and the matter of trying to find some beer.'

'You heading over West?' a new voice from behind Cougar said. 'You'd better get yourself a bodyguard.'

'Would you care for the job?' Cougar asked humorlessly as he turned, but his face broke into a wide grin as he recognized his taunter. 'Dallas McGee!'

'So you haven't forgotten me!' The two men shook hands warmly, Cougar looking McGee up and down with pleasure.

'Where in the world have you been?' Cougar asked. 'And what are you doing out here on the trail to nowhere?'

'Well, Carroll — I've just been wandering, breaking women's hearts and a few men's jaws,' the Texan replied. His own grin was infectious. Lanky, red-haired, his one remaining good eye twinkled brightly. He wore well-rubbed chaps, run-down-at-the-heel boots, and a gray shirt that was fraying at the collar.

Cougar said, 'Guess who I've got out in that wagon. Calvin D'Arcy.'

'D'Arcy! Now there's a coincidence for you. Crook's three old white scouts running into each other at this fly-speck outpost. Which reminds me, I saw old Deerfoot a month or so back. He took a bullet in the spine. He keeps mainly to a chair on the porch of a hotel down in Tucson.'

'Too bad,' Cougar, who had genuinely liked the old Ute Indian scout, said. There was a vague uneasiness fluttering around in the back of his skull. Life was full of coincidences, but as Dallas McGee said, this one was quite remarkable . . . if it was coincidence.

'Yeah,' Dallas was saying, 'it comes to us all in the end. Deerfoot doesn't seem to mind much, though he's drinking a lot. Too much. Did I hear you asking about horses, Cougar?' he said, changing the subject. 'I can come by five or six head of good riding stock.'

'You can? If so, four would do us fine, Dallas. One each for me and D'Arcy, couple of spares. Assuming they're better than dog meat.'

'They'll do,' Dallas promised. 'I know you were always one for having the best horseflesh possible under you, so they might not be quite up to your standard. That is, they may be a little stubby for you. They're got a lot of mustang blood in them, but they're desert horses and you know that mustang-bred means they've got stamina. The man who owns them is named Yount — I can take you out to his place. Where did you say you were intending to go, Cougar?'

'West by south — White Mesa country. Do you know it?'

'Yes I do and damn me!' Dallas said, taking off his hat to scratch at his red hair. The one-eyed man told him, 'I'm heading that direction myself, Carroll. The three of us can ride together. Just like old times.'

'The problem is,' Cougar had to tell him, 'D'Arcy and I got into a little scrape back upcountry. He got shot up pretty good.'

'Don't tell me! What was it all about?'

'I'll tell you later,' Cougar said although he had no intention of going into all the details. He would just tell Dallas that they had been jumped by outlaws — that should satisfy his curiosity. 'And,' Cougar said with a heavy sigh, 'we won't be able to ride along with you anyway, Dallas. There's other complications.'

Dallas appeared disappointed. After all, almost any company was welcome company on the empty, hostile desert. And old friends to travel with made for good riding. 'Whatever you say, Carroll. But just what is it that — ?'

The little bell over the door tinkled and Ellen White, back-lighted by the morning sky came in, still blinded by the transition from harsh sunlight to sudden murkiness. She stood there blinking, looking very small and quite appealing. Dallas McGee smiled.

'Is that the complication, Carroll?' he asked with a soft whistle. 'Now, just who is she? She's looking this way, partner. Is she your woman?'

'No,' Cougar said uncomfortably, a little too strongly. 'I'll explain all of this when we have the time. For now just let me grab something for D'Arcy to drink and we can talk to the man about the horses.'

'Sure, Carroll. Meantime, I've got my spare horse out back. Don't have a saddle, do you?'

'No. We lost those too.'

'No matter. I can borrow one from Bob here,' he said, nodding toward the bald-headed man. His eyes, however, were still fixed on Ellen White, measuring her, and enjoying what he saw. Well, Cougar thought with the slightest tinge of jealousy, a jealousy he had no right to shelter, you couldn't blame a man for looking.

'I appreciate this,' Cougar said, deliberately turning his back to Ellen, who still stood, appearing slightly puzzled, watching them across the floor. 'Dallas, if you don't mind my asking, what in the world are you doing riding out this way?'

McGee's eye was slightly sheepish. 'Hell, Cougar — you see these rags I'm dressed in. I used to be a sharp dresser, they say. Now I've got nothing but my horses and my Colt. I stayed too long in too many worthless places handing what I had over to too many sweet-smelling useless women, drinking, gambling, sinking too low. Remember that big land company deal I used to brag about around the campfire in the old days? How I was going to stake my savings on it and make a fortune while the rest of you ate dust and dodged arrows? That turned into a joke. Payback for my bragging, I suppose. It blew up in my face and I lost everything I'd saved. Hell,' he muttered, 'I thought if I could hook up with General Crook he might be willing to take on an old over-the-hill scout.'

Cougar said slowly. 'Damn sorry to hear your ship didn't come in, Dallas. I mean it.'

But — how in God's name had Dallas McGee guessed where to find General Crook?

'Let me buy you a cup of cider,' Cougar said, throwing an arm around Dallas McGee's shoulder, 'and then let's say hello to D'Arcy.'

Cougar was silent as McGee climbed up into the wagon to greet D'Arcy and the two old plains fighters swapped stories. Cougar hated to admit it, but he was suspicious and worried. He knew there was nothing to it, couldn't be. He'd known Dallas McGee too long and too well. But by God it was a hell of a coincidence to run across him out in the far reaches and discover that he was heading to their own destination.

Cougar hadn't forgotten what D'Arcy had said. You could buy a hell of a lot of men in this territory, at this time, with American dollars ... or Prussian gold. Cougar still carried some of that gold he had taken from one American who had volunteered to betray his country. The gold, true, was minted in Denver, but it had passed through foreign hands, he now believed. The country was young, wide, tentatively controlled. Other nations not so land-wealthy would not be adverse to carving new colonies out of the West. They had tried it before and would likely try it again.

But Dallas! Cougar felt ashamed of himself for even considering it — maybe he was being infected by the vast yet insubstantial threat, finding conspiracies everywhere. He shook away his fleeting doubts. Not Dallas McGee, ever. He could not be the man sent to assassinate General Crook, giving the Indians the sign that the great uprising was to begin . . . Still, it was the damndest of coincidences.

Leaving D'Arcy to swelter in the wagon while Dr White and Ellen waited wearing grim expressions, Cougar and Dallas rode off in the opposite direction, finding the rancher, Yount, home at his shanty looking hopeful and desperate at the same time. The land was harsh and he obviously had little cash money.

Cougar and McGee looked over Yount's horses. They were more sound than Carroll Cougar had expected, and well worth what the rancher was asking.

Cougar selected a sorrel with an angry look in its eye and spirit in its heart. It took some time to saddle and bridle the three-year-old and it would take some time to get the scrappy animal used to having a man aboard.

'He's hard to get started, Mr Cougar,' Yount told him, 'but once you get him going he'll stay under you all day.'

'He'll do fine. I didn't come looking for a schoolteacher's horse,' Cougar replied from the sorrel's back, and Yount grunted his appreciation of the sentiment.

The horse he judged second best he intended for D'Arcy's prime mount, a deep-chested gray with a notched ear. For his own second horse he chose a buckskin with a black mane and tail

— eight years old but long and strappy-looking. A bright-eyed little pinto was to be D'Arcy's second mount. Perhaps expecting script, Yount's eyes brightened as well when Cougar paid him with sun-bright, newly minted gold.

With the remuda in tow Cougar and D'Arcy headed back toward the dumpy little town where D'Arcy and the Whites waited with the wagon. Dallas was very silent as they rode onward. The sky was clear except for a few clouds as delicate and white as a lady's lace. Finally Cougar asked him, 'What is it, Dallas? Something's eating you.'

'I'm trying to calculate whether to speak up or not,' the one-eyed Texan said worriedly.

'There's no point in holding it in, is there?'

'I don't know.' Dallas said, 'I told you that I ran into Deerfoot down in Tucson, didn't I?'

'Yes.'

Dallas thought it through again, made up his mind, and with a shrug reported, 'Deerfoot told me that a good friend of his, another Ute — can't recall his name — saw Solon Reineke about a month ago.'

From the corner of his eye Dallas saw Cougar stiffen slightly. Cougar's face became a hard mask. Yes, he still felt the same way about the outlaw.

'Where did he see him?' the big man asked.

'Down around Alamo Banks. You recall the place?'

'I do. That's where you got yourself cut up, isn't it?'

'You know it is. Apache lance should've gone through my throat. His pony must've stumbled. All I lost is this,' Dallas said, touching his eyepatch.

Neither man spoke again for a long while as they rode slowly across the red and gray land only here and there dusted with the pale green of new grass. The horses' hoofs swished over the sandy soil. The sorrel, still contentious, side-hopped from time to time, challenging Cougar to control him. Besides the grass that the recent rain had tried to bring to life, nothing grew between there and the way station except, only here and there, yellow-flowering thorny mesquite and clumps of nopal cactus.

Another silent mile passed under their horses' hoofs before Dallas McGee said, 'He seen her too.'

'Who?' Cougar asked although somehow he already knew what the answer would be.

'Quiet Star. She got off that reservation for good, finally. She's running wild.'

'So?'

'So, Cougar — she's changed. Maybe the reservation changed her, I don't know. The Ute says that Quiet Star wants to kill herself some white men now. All white men. She's become a hateful thing. She's crazy with it. Someone . . . something has made her into a vengeful woman.'

'What do I care?' Cougar asked. The bright silver disc on the necklace that the girl-child had once made for him glinted in the sunlight.

'Maybe you don't. I just thought I should tell you. If you ever see her again, Cougar, you might want to remember that. Because if you ever do happen to meet you might have to kill her before she can kill you.'

7

What Cougar learned from Dallas McGee on the ride back to the stage station from Yount's ranch was that the threat of coming war was no secret at all in New Mexico and Arizona. No one down there knew the extent of the plot, and of course they had no knowledge of the attempt to be made on General Crook's life or its implications, but they had heard that it was going to be an all-out holy war by the Apaches and maybe the Comanches, and that by itself was plenty to scare off many settlers into getting out of the territories while there was still time.

What if they knew that the Mexicans desperately wanted that land back and that European influences were once again at work on the continent, trying to undermine the young nation? Fear might turn to panic, Cougar knew, and if in fact Crook were assassinated, panic could turn to complete chaos.

'Do you happen to read German?' Cougar asked as they dipped down through a dry, willow-line watercourse. He was thinking of the mysterious letter he had captured from the ambusher along with the gold — and the inexplicable human tooth that had been in the chamois sack the ambusher had been carrying. All he got for an answer was, predictably, a puzzled stare and a 'Huh?' from Dallas, who looked at him as if Cougar had been smoking jimson weed.

'Never mind,' Cougar said, and the Texan shrugged at the out-of-the-blue inquiry.

D'Arcy had managed to pry himself out of the wagon on the urging of sheer impatience and when they reached the wagon they found him leaning against the tailgate, his shirt still showing a huge dried bloodstain, his face pale from the loss of the bodily fluid. If D'Arcy had grown understandably impatient, Dr White and Ellen were even more so.

'I must say, Mr Cougar,' White said, 'there seems to be no haste at all in your movements. You know that I am expected urgently.'

Cougar didn't even dignify that comment with a glance as he tied the horses up to the hitch rail beside the wagon. To D'Arcy he said, 'You'd better get back into that bed. That's the only way you're going to heal enough to do us any good.'

The narrow scout grinned back feebly: 'Well, I would, Cougar — I'm just not sure I can make it back up now that I've slid out.'

'We'll see to that, Calvin. You're getting back into bed, and don't give me an argument unless you feel like stepping on to that gray horse's back.'

D'Arcy eyed the gray horse, its muscles twitching beneath its hide as it stood at the rail. Its evil eye found D'Arcy, and Calvin smiled. 'No, sir. I don't believe I wish to try that just now.

Before we leave, though, Cougar, would you see if they've got any apples or carrots inside the store . . . parsnips, maybe? I once had a big roan that was partial to parsnips. I want to make friends with that demon before I swing aboard.'

Cougar found some of each for D'Arcy and threw them into a burlap sack for the patient to use as peace offerings for the big gray horse. When the wagon rolled out of town, D'Arcy, despite his promise to return to his sickbed, was perched on the tailgate of the wagon, feeding the horse tidbits as they went, trying to form a friendship with his new ally.

At a cattail-clotted pond where they watered the horses, Cougar offered to let the girl ride the buckskin if she liked, and to his surprise, she accepted despite her father's disapproving glare. A well brought-up lady did not ride astride and they had no such thing as a side-saddle. When they started on again, then, Ellen, sitting her saddle lightly, rode beside Cougar, Dallas trailing, D'Arcy still teasing and lecturing the gray horse, occasionally giving it a carrot or a parsnip to cement their relationship.

The wheels of the wagon creaked, the trace chains jangled. The horses shuffled patiently onward as a long red mesa appeared before them. There was a bother of gnats around their faces from time to time, but the day was mostly pleasant with an intermittent light breeze flowing down from the north. Dallas sang off-key as he rode; D'Arcy laughed from time to time at the antics of the gray horse, which now had learned where its treats were to come from and was growing more demanding, sulking when nuzzling D'Arcy's hand didn't result in instant appetite gratification. The pinto, bright-eyed and carefree, drifted along behind on its tether rope, not caring one way or the other what the other horses or the two-legged creatures did.

The girl in the thin white blouse that

the wind pushed attractively against her breasts, hat on a thong down her back, and a divided black skirt, rode along easily beside Cougar. She was silent, but her eyes were alert and inquisitive. Now and then a smile caused by some secret thought parted her full lips.

A more serious look came into her eyes as she asked Cougar, 'We really are in a lot of danger out here, aren't we?'

'A lot,' Cougar replied honestly. Ellen knew about the Indian situation, of course, but nothing had yet been said about the trailing white ambushers. 'If you can shoot,' Cougar told her seriously, 'it would be a very good idea to carry a gun.'

'Father doesn't believe in guns,' she said a little wearily.

'I somehow didn't think he would,' Cougar said without emphasis.

The wagon road skirted a long, craggy hill clogged with fields of nopal cactus. Cougar automatically searched the knoll with his eyes. She watched him closely.

'You're kind-of a funny man,' Ellen said and Cougar half-turned in the saddle to return her speculative look.

'Am I? How do you mean?'

'Well, you act so mean and rough,' she said, 'but there's a streak of tenderness in you as well.'

'You never saw any tenderness in me,' he muttered. The girl made him uncomfortable in a way he could not define.

'Sure I have. Like the way you took care of your friend.'

'That's only duty, Ellen. What was I to do, leave D'Arcy?'

'No.' She shook her head. 'That wasn't only duty, Cougar. I saw you with him, saw your concern, remember? Cougar — I think I'm starting to figure you out.'

'And so?'

'And so, when I do, you may find you have your hands full.' With that, Ellen spun the buckskin away, heeling it hard for a few hundred yards before she slowed it again to a walk, remaining at a distance from the rest of them.

Dallas McGee, drawing up beside his friend, asked, 'And just what was that about, Cougar? What'd you do, offend the girl?' He nodded toward Ellen.

'I don't know what it was about, Dallas. I just don't know.'

'Well,' Dallas said philosophically, 'women — they got their ways. I don't think mortal man is supposed to understand what they're up to.'

Cougar wasn't listening. His mind had returned again to something else. The one thing that haunted him. The one thing he had never totally come to grips with. 'You were there, right, Dallas?'

McGee knew what the big man meant: *Carlina*. 'You know I was there, Cougar. You, me, D'Arcy, those two enlisted men — I can't recollect their names — and Deerfoot.'

'And Solon Reineke.'

'And Reineke.' Dallas nodded.

'So tell me, Dallas — '

'Cougar! I can't.'

'I mean it,' Cougar said. 'Tell me again just what you saw. Heard.' His eyes were lighted harshly, fixed on the distances where the land folded and convoluted and the dry grass, dusted with red earth, suffered under a hot sun and the saw-toothed hills drew steadily nearer.

'All right,' Dallas said heavily. 'We were camped in Guapo Valley . . . Why are you asking me, Cougar? You were there. You know what happened. Why ask me to bring it all up again? You're just hurting yourself.' Cougar did not answer and so after a deep breath, Dallas went on, touching the tip of his tongue to his dry lips.

'You and Deerfoot,' Dallas continued, 'had gone out chasing a mule deer buck. We needed some meat. Dusk had settled. Everything was kinda deep purple-blue across the valley. There was a ground fog rising. The fire was glowing pretty. When it all happened I was already rolled up in my bed. I sat up quick, but too late to do anything.'

'What did you see? What did you hear?'

'Ah, Cougar, why . . . OK. I heard two shots, jumped out of my bed. Solon Reineke was running away hard and . . . Carlina was dead. D'Arcy was yelling at the top of his lungs, 'Get him! He shot her!' Reineke got himself lost in the dark and we never found him.'

'Two shots?' Cougar said. 'Carlina was only shot once.'

'I don't know. I guess someone fired back. Maybe D'Arcy.'

'He didn't.'

'Well, hell, I don't know then, Cougar,' Dallas said, adjusting his eyepatch. 'Maybe Solon shot twice and missed once. Hard to see how he could have at that range, but maybe he was shook up. I don't see that one shot or two matters that much. Solon Reineke killed Carlina. We all saw it.'

'Yes, I know,' Cougar said with dark bitterness.

'Is that why you're heading out there,

Cougar? Is it Solon Reineke that you're after?'

'Yes, it's Reineke.'

'I see.' Dallas was thoughtful again as they rode side by side. 'You asked me a kind-of funny question, Cougar. About do I read German . . . '

'So?'

'I don't know. It was just an awful funny question. There has to be something you're not telling me. That's all right — maybe you don't think I need to know. But I was thinking . . . Reineke, ain't that a German name?' And then Dallas slowed his horse to leave Cougar to ride on alone with his sullen and confused thoughts.

It was already turning toward dusk and Cougar had begun to look for a likely campsite when Dallas approached him again, his horse lifted into a canter before he reined in alongside.

'Did you see 'em, Cougar? We've got trouble.'

Cougar, whose eyes had been looking westward for a sign of water and grass indicating a decent camp ground, now looked back in the direction Dallas was indicating. 'Damn,' Cougar muttered. A long line of riders was visible against the skyline to the southeast. 'Mexicans,' he said, stating the obvious. Their outsized sombreros were clearly visible and the excessive silver on their saddles, glinting in the late sunlight, marked them for men from across the border.

'Would they be looking for us, do you think?' Dallas asked.

'You know they must be,' Cougar answered. A wagon, probably full of supplies, was theirs for the taking, along with six horses. And if they spotted Ellen . . . It's us they're after. They are probably just talking it over still, wondering if it's worth the risk.'

He said nothing to Dallas about the other reason these men might be trailing along. That the vaqueros could possibly be going West to join the army that was supposed to be gathering there to do battle with General Crook's forces.

'They're holding their distance,' Dallas commented.

'For the time being.' But it wasn't dark yet. And that was when any would-be raiders would probably prefer to descend upon them.

Then Dallas said something with a touch of uncharacteristic nervousness: 'Directly back of us there's another party of men. You can just make out their dust.'

'I know they're there,' Cougar said calmly.

'Damn all, Cougar!' Dallas McGee suddenly exploded. 'If you don't trust me, fine. I'll cut out on my own, but something sure as hell is going on around here, and I don't feel like risking my life over something I don't even understand. You're holding out on me, old friend, and I don't know why.'

So Cougar told him. There was nothing else to do. Dallas was right. He was risking his life by being with their small party. When he had finished his explanation, Dallas sat his saddle in deep silence.

'So that's how it is,' he said at last.

'That's how it is. If you want to ride out now, I couldn't blame you.'

'Hell no, I'm not going to cut and run.' Dallas grinned. 'I just needed to know what sort of ball I was attending.'

The Mexicans continued to follow them as they moved onward, but eventually they were lost in the deep twilight. When they could travel on no farther safely, Cougar rode back to the wagon and told Dr White, 'We'd better stake out a dry camp. Atop that rocky knoll, I think.'

Dr White shouted back from the wagon bench. The horses can't pull that slope! We'll have to carry up what we need. Why not camp on flat ground?'

'Because we can carry up what we need — food, water, blankets, and ammunition — easier than we can keep mounted men from riding through our camp,' Cougar answered. 'Have a look behind you.'

At his pointing finger, White looked back and saw the horsemen moving like ghosts through the twilight purple. 'What are they? Indians?' he asked.

'Mexicans, we think, but it doesn't matter who they might be. We have no idea what their intentions might be and the high ground is much safer.'

'All right,' White said, finally understanding. He glanced at his daughter. Ellen sat beside him on the seat, young, small and quite pretty. White seemed to be beginning to comprehend the sort of situation he had brought her into.

They set up camp as quickly and as quietly as possible. Cougar and Dallas never put their rifles down. They watched, unspeaking, as sunset dimmed to crimson, blinked bright briefly, and then faded across the dark land.

Ellen sat quietly on a flat volcanic rock atop the small knoll. Dr White moved about aimlessly in nervous agitation. D'Arcy, who had borne the discomfort of being carried up the hill in grim silence, groaned now and then

130

with pain. He had been seated on a blanket beside a large, pocked boulder.

To Cougar, Calvin D'Arcy seemed to be getting no better. His fever remained high. Dr White had told Cougar, but not D'Arcy of course, that he still believed the arm was going to have to be taken off if the man were to survive. They were an unhappy and nearly defenseless little group. Cougar, studying White, found himself wondering why a man of his caliber would ever volunteer for the rugged wilderness life of an army surgeon. Cougar had known a few such surgeons in his time, and they had, almost without exception, been men of deep courage, knowing they might find themselves unarmed in the field trying to perform surgery under septic conditions and even under fire.

Was there more behind Dr White's decision to come West than Cougar had been told?

He turned his attention to Ellen as he sat, rifle propped up between his knees in the near-darkness. He could ask her to tell him more about White, but he thought he would get no new answers. She was an intensely loyal woman, and, he thought now, stronger than she had seemed at first. Was she, perhaps, the glue that held their little family together and not Dr White himself?

'There's someone creeping around down in that gully,' Dallas whispered, and behind them he could hear D'Arcy gently cock his Winchester.

'Are you sure?' Cougar asked, seeing nothing himself.

'I've still got one good eye, Carroll. He's over there, near that clump of sage. Just beyond those twin boulders.'

'How many do you make out?' Cougar strained his eyes against the darkness. Damn! He should have been keeping better watch himself instead of sitting there worrying about Ellen.

'One's all I saw,' Dallas whispered. 'Do you want me to go down and take a look?'

'I guess I will, Dallas,' Cougar said

softly. He handed his friend his Spencer repeater and took his razor-edged bowie from its sheath. 'I guess it's my place to have a look.'

8

Cougar slipped into the darkness beyond the camp with the long-bladed knife in his hand, his feet as silent as a big cat's as he moved across rocks and sand using only the last light of purple dusk to guide him. There would not be a moon until close to morning and the stars seemed thin and worn behind the haze of the desert sky.

Whoever was below had a terrible surprise in store for him. The big man was coming; the cougar was tracking. There would be blood spilled when Cougar embraced his enemy.

To Ellen, who had watched him as he stole out of camp, it was like watching a shadow pass through shadows, his footfalls whispers, his bulk fading against the darkness surrounding him. She bit at her lower lip and started when her father placed an arm around her shoulders.

She spoke not at all to Cougar as he passed; she knew there were hunting men out there and instinct sealed her lips.

There was a ground fog as light as babies' breath against Cougar's cheek. He felt his way carefully down the slope, not wanting to dislodge a single pebble. He moved in increments, pausing every few steps to crouch and study what lay around him in the night.

The dim stars cast muted shadows against the earth. The canyon bottom itself was like a dark river. When he reached it he still had heard nothing at all except his own tight breathing and the faint sounds of his boots against the sand.

But there was a hunter out there; Cougar could nearly feel his presence like the slight warmth of a body nearby . . . but where? He crouched now in a stand of laurel-leaf sumac and sage, scenting the familiar, pungent odor of the chaparral. Still nothing moved or made a muted sound against the hovering night. Cougar held his bowie knife beside his thigh so that there was no chance of the feeble starlight glinting off of it.

Something rustled down the canyon, a shuttling sound like a rattlesnake over leaves and Cougar felt his muscles tighten in response. His heart began to beat a little faster. It seemed that it rose and swelled in his chest. He still did not move at all, but only waited, and after a few minutes he was again rewarded with the slight echo of a tiny rustling sound. A man moving through brush? A prowling bobcat?

Nothing moved as Cougar bunched himself into a tighter ball of muscle and honed steel, his legs tensed so that they were nearly cramped under him, his hand knotted like an iron band around the stag-horn handle of his bowie knife.

Then the *thing* sprang from the brush, making only an angry hissing sound before its body collided with Cougar's. Cougar's knife slashed out and a scream ripped the night.

The attacker tried to hammer at Cougar with his hand, which was fisted around the handle of a pistol, but Cougar caught his wrist as he fell on to his back, tugging his assailant after him.

Simultaneously, the big scout drove a knee into his attacker's groin and slashed out again with the deadly blade of the big bowie. Steel met the flesh of the other man's throat with deadly savagery and there was a trapped, gurgling sound as warm fluid flooded Cougar's face and hand.

Then the attacker lay still, blood soaking into the arroyo sand, and Cougar rolled his body aside, retreating quickly to the shelter of the brush where he panted, watching and waiting. There may have been more of them out there and Cougar was taking no chances.

The cicadas began to sing and a rising breeze to stir the brush around him. Still no one came following the dead man. Cougar rose and moved carefully to the body of the man he had killed and crouched low, examining him.

They had never met before, nor was he a Mexican.

Who, then, was he? *Who?* The question was frustrating. He must have been another of the men who had been tracking them since Twin Creek. Maybe had grown impatient with the long trail and decided to strike here and now and have done with it. A desperate attempt to stop Cougar and D'Arcy. But then, where were his partners? Simple impatience could not explain the man's motives, whoever he was. Whoever he had been.

Cougar patted the man down, finding nothing that seemed of significance. He wore a silver and copper bracelet, an unusual piece of jewelry, with the strands of both metals woven together. Cougar removed it, tugged his gunbelt from under him, slinging it over his shoulder. Then, after a few more silent, watching moments, he started back toward the camp on the rocky knoll.

He whistled very softly — two tones — before he re-entered the camp and D'Arcy answered with his own whistle. Then Cougar was in the camp and to his astonishment Ellen was in his arms, shuddering.

She drew back suddenly and Cougar knew that it was the blood on him that had driven her away.

'Down there . . . ?' she began to ask, but she had no need to finish the question, nor was there any need for Cougar to answer. She looked at his bloody face and shirt and the captured gunbelt across his shoulder and knew that he had killed.

'How many?' was D'Arcy's whispered question.

'One,' Cougar said and a puzzled silence followed. Cougar knew what D'Arcy was thinking — why one man alone unless he was simply scouting out their camp? But if that was so, why then would he choose to attack Cougar?

'I suppose now we can — ' Dr White

said very loudly and Cougar hissed back at him.

'I suppose now we can just keep quiet the rest of the night! I'll stand guard. You've got second watch, Dallas,' Cougar said, and then he ambled toward the highest of the dark, jumbled rocks towering above the camp, and, with his Spencer rifle in hand, he sat down to endure three long hours of night watch.

The enemy was out there, but what did he want? And when would he come in force? Perhaps they were waiting for their small party to get farther out on to the approaching desert where accidents were many and discovery rare. Cougar could not outguess them just now; he had no answers. He could only sit and glare out at the sullen night, his big .56 repeater across his lap.

Now and then he thought of Ellen in the large emptiness of the long night. Could that woman possibly be falling for him? How could such a thing be — she a well-raised lady and he a big, uncouth grizzly of a man? He thought of her slender body against his as he returned to camp. It had probably been only relief that had pushed her into his arms. Yet, for just a moment there he had felt . . . well, thought he had felt, something beyond that. Something inexplicable, probably imagined. And something, if real, he definitely was not prepared for. Not now, not now. He was still trying to complete his love for Carlina.

He tried to push Ellen from his mind and with difficulty managed it. He returned to his troubled brooding and troubled puzzling, to staring against the dark, threatening curtain of the desert night.

Cougar, using the slow swing of the Dipper's handle for his clock as the constellation rotated around Polaris, awakened Dallas about three hours later to stand his watch. He, himself, turned into his bed immediately, dropping off to a deep, dreamless sleep. Many men had wondered at his ability to do that, about the wisdom of it, but Cougar had the time-tested capacity to sleep deeply and still have the ability to come alert at once. No, his body needed sleep badly and it did come rapidly, but his senses were never totally unconscious. And so it was that when Dallas came past him in the early morning to wake D'Arcy to the darkness for his shift, Cougar heard the footsteps, Dallas's murmuring, and watched as D'Arcy rose with Dallas's help.

And it seemed to Cougar that the two men whispered together for just a little time too long. Dallas turned slightly toward Cougar's bed, studying it. Cougar saw the one-eyed man shake his head and say something else in a throttled whisper. Then the two men separated in the night, D'Arcy hobbling toward his lookout position.

Cougar went back to sleep again. This time he did dream: the bad old dream of Carlina lying dead on her blankets, her clothes half torn off, the blood smearing her beautiful body with a sickly maroon stain.

The first glint of sunlight hadn't yet darted through the flimsy clouds in the eastern sky when Cougar first heard movement that brought him awake in the silent, dour camp. In the cold gray of morning D'Arcy sat shivering with a blanket around his shoulders, eyes deep set and red. Dallas fidgeted nervously with his revolver, wiping it with a cloth but not actually cleaning it. Dr White, appearing several years older than he had just days ago, had tried to slick back his hair and dust off his dark suit, but ineffectively. Only Ellen looked up to the challenge of the new morning, but even her face was drawn, her lips drawn down unhappily.

Cougar rolled out of his bed and got to his feet in one swift movement. The others watched him silently, almost without expression.

'Any sign of them?' Cougar asked D'Arcy as he rolled up his blankets.

'None. It seems to me, Cougar, that

they might have just ridden on past us in the night. Hoofs on sand wouldn't have made enough sound to draw our attention.'

'That could be. Maybe we weren't of as much interest to the Mexicans as we thought. They might have just been giving us the eye.' Cougar stood, hands on hips, looking out at the world around them as the sky paled with the coming dawn.

'You mean they didn't know who we were?' D'Arcy asked.

'Exactly. How would they? If they were soldiers recruited for another mission and not simply bandits, they might have taken notice of us and investigated, seeing nothing that interested them enough to start a fuss; they would have continued on to another place where they had more urgent business.'

'Like the White Mountains,' D'Arcy said grimly.

'Like the White Mountains where General Crook is holed up, still not even knowing that he is being gradually surrounded.'

Morning rolled on and still they saw no one as the sky brightened with the colors of new dawn and they made their way back down the rocky knoll to the wagon and their picketed horses. Cougar was already in the saddle of his sorrel when he noticed that the doctor still hadn't come down from the night camp. Ellen White was sitting alone on the wagon bench.

'Where's your father?' he asked the girl, who sat, hands clasped between her knees, looking out at the gray desert ahead of them.

'He's still up there.' She nodded. 'It is a spiritual moment.'

'It's what? Do you mean he's up there praying?'

'It is time for him to meditate and contact his spiritual connection,' she replied with a weak smile.

'Ellen, I don't understand what you're telling me,' Cougar said frankly. 'It's time that we were going — there isn't time to stop and commune with whatever spirits you are talking about.'

'Nevertheless,' the girl said, 'Father feels that he must. That is what he is doing.' Ellen kept her gaze from Cougar's face.

'That's a part of the rituals in this church he had, is it?' Cougar asked, looking up toward the crest of the knoll. White still had not appeared.

'Yes . . . ' Ellen murmured, 'a part of it.'

Dallas McGee had ridden up to the wagon, his horse sidestepping with morning friskiness. 'What's up?' he asked Cougar. 'Are we going to roll this morning?'

'Soon,' Cougar answered. 'The doctor is busy with some sort of spiritual communion.'

'Huh?' Dallas looked toward the knoll, frowning.

'Never mind. We'll be on our way soon — one way or the other.'

'All right. Cougar — how about if I ride out ahead a little, see if I can cut some sign?' Dallas suggested.

'Sure,' Cougar said grouchily. He wasn't angry with Dallas, but this business with White was annoying him. Why couldn't the man do his communing at night when they had nothing else to do but sleep? 'That's an idea, Dallas. Ride on out a little way, but don't get too far ahead of us.' With a nod and a tip of his hat to Ellen, Dallas heeled his horse and left them, taking the first few hundred yards at a gallop to take the edge off his horse's ambition.

Cougar watched Dallas go and then told Ellen, 'I'll give your father five more minutes. The day's going to get too hot for us soon to just be sitting here, waiting. How long does this meditating usually take him?'

'There's no telling. It depends on when his spirit leader arrives,' Ellen said, with embarrassment flaming her cheeks. It must, Cougar thought, have been terrible for her back in St Louis. Whatever religion her father practiced it sure wasn't strict Methodism or any other sort of worship Cougar was aware of. He had turned his horse's head and started walking it slowly away when he heard Ellen gasp, and turning he saw her hands at her mouth in horror.

'What is it?' Cougar asked, his hand going to his gun butt.

She pointed with a trembling hand. 'That! Where did that come from?'

What she had seen was the twisted bracelet Cougar had placed on his own wrist for convenience, the woven copper and silver piece of jewelry he had taken from the man he had killed the night before.

'Last night,' he explained. 'The man who was down in the gully, looking for us. He was wearing this. I didn't want to shove it in a pocket, but I thought it might give us a clue as to who he was.'

'And then you . . . '

'And I killed him. He tried to kill me, Ellen,' Cougar said. 'Just what is it that suddenly disturbed you?' he asked, looking at the bracelet himself now.

'You've seen this before somewhere, haven't you?'

'I was just wondering about it,' she lied. She lied so transparently that Cougar didn't bother to call her on it. She knew he had seen through the lie. Apparently she hadn't had much practice at bending the truth. She wasn't very good at it.

He started to demand an answer. It could be important, but then he heard a shout from the hill and, turning, saw Dr White with his arms held wildly aloft, stumbling down the slope toward them.

'Now what?' Cougar grumbled. 'What in the hell is going on?' he asked White more loudly. 'You act like you've seen something frightening.'

'I have seen it all,' Dr White babbled. Perspiration beaded on his forehead and trickled down toward his eyes. His expression was a mixture of fear and exhilaration. 'I have seen it all — now I know that we are going the right way.'

Cougar looked to Ellen for clarification, but she only shook her head minutely. The minister walked to where she sat on the wagon bench and bowed his face into her upturned palms. His entire body was trembling; he seemed exhausted.

Cougar knew he was going to get nothing else from the man and so, gritting his teeth, he angrily turned his mount away. D'Arcy, grinning, was seated on the tailgate of the wagon, holding the gray horse's bridle.

'Did you hear that?' Cougar asked.

'Most of it.'

'Just what kind of madman are we traveling with?'

'I couldn't tell you, Cougar,' D'Arcy said with dry humor. 'I'd have to meditate on that.'

Cougar lifted a warning finger, let it drop again and then, as Dr White started his team forward with a lurch, he himself rode ahead of the wagon to try to join up with Dallas, leaving D'Arcy — rifle in hand — to ride with the wagon.

Cougar found Dallas afoot in a dry

wash, crouched down against the sand. The redhead looked up as Cougar approached, cutting a trail through the dry cattails there.

'Find anything?' Cougar asked.

'You might want to have your own look,' Dallas said, rising to dust his hands off. 'But what I make of it is that the Mexicans appear to have ridden around us and then on through.' He pointed toward the dun-colored, saw-toothed mountains in that direction. They could just be made out through the blue haze of the desert morning. No riders were visible on the horizon. 'You can make out some of their trail back a way. There were maybe twenty or thirty of them. At an estimate. But the others — '

'What others?' Cougar asked sharply.

'You'd have to tell me, Cougar. I cut the sign of maybe three, maybe up to six men — the land is lava rock and sand, it don't read well — kind of making a lazy circle around us. I was thinking maybe they were the men who've been stalking you and D'Arcy all along.'

'Maybe just drifting outlaws looking for the main chance,' Cougar suggested, not believing it himself.

'It could be.' The one-eyed man shrugged. 'Whoever it is, though, they're not riding straight to anywhere — not like these Mexican vaqueros are. They're just hanging around aimlessly.'

Not so aimlessly, Cougar guessed. He thought that Dallas was probably right. These were the same men who had been tracking himself and D'Arcy all along, since his home ranch. They were still being hunted. Only the idea that they would have to face three armed and knowledgeable men was keeping them off. But Dallas had said he thought there could be up to six of them now. Maybe they had hired on some other men . . . and if they found still more gunhands to swell their numbers, what then?

'We can't do a thing but keep going, stay alert,' Dallas said.

'Not a thing,' Cougar was forced to reluctantly agree.

The longer this went on, the more he regretted having let D'Arcy talk him into this even with the nation seeming to need him, even with a request from the President himself. If it weren't for the hope of finding Solon Reineke, he might still have refused. But there was that chance, and find Reineke Cougar would.

Finally find him and extract the full price for the killer's unholy crime. He could do no more to honor the memory of Carlina's love — and no less.

9

The party entered true desert that day. The heat veils rose like smoke from the white, rolling ground. Only mesquite and smokewood, cholla cactus, and here and there a bedraggled, dead cottonwood tree broke the barrenness.

They followed the only trail that seemed passable by wagon. Even there the wheels cut deep grooves in the sand. The horses labored on, their heads bowed. The sun was a branding iron on their backs. Cougar was already worrying about water. The barrels strapped to the wagon wouldn't last long, not with the stock they now possessed.

At times D'Arcy seemed to get better, to come more alert, but then he would fall off into the depths of pain and numbness of before. Sometimes when Cougar, lagging to check on his friend's well-being, spoke to Calvin D'Arcy his thoughts became temporarily disordered and he spoke in words that were nearly incoherent. Then with a crooked, apologetic smile, D'Arcy would wave a hand in frustration and fall back against his blankets in the heated wagon.

'I believe I can save his arm,' Dr White confided to Cougar at a stop where the two men stood in the scattered shade of tall mesquite bushes, insects swarming around their faces.

'But?' Cougar prompted, seeing the gloom in the doctor's eyes.

'What I have in mind will save his arm, but it will never be any good again. I can't do anything about the nerve damage. The arm will just be a dangling, useless thing.' There was genuine sadness in the doctor's voice. Cougar turned his head to look back at the wagon where D'Arcy lay.

'Does he know that?'

'He asked me,' Dr White said with an apologetic shrug. 'What was I to do?

Lie? I told him what the situation was likely to become. Yes, Mr D'Arcy knows.'

Cougar sauntered very slowly toward D'Arcy, the gravelly desert soil crunching beneath his boots as he moved. He found D'Arcy beside the covered wagon, standing in the thin shade it cast.

Before Cougar could form a single word, D'Arcy lifted a silencing hand. 'Yes, I know about it, Cougar. The doctor was honest with me. Still, I thank you. This could have turned out much worse if it weren't for you.'

'Yes, that's right. It could have been even worse,' Cougar replied. Then only briefly he placed a hand on D'Arcy's shoulder. His friend wanted no sympathy, nor did Cougar know how to offer it to him.

★ ★ ★

The tiny town was called Triumph. It looked flimsy and weathered as if it didn't stand much of a chance of lasting on the hard desert, but to the travelers it was like an oasis when they reached it the following evening. Trail-dusty, alkali-covered, any sheltering, shaded place where they could replenish water and supplies was a godsend.

They reached it at sundown with the western sky like a water-color wash of dull red and deep purple. Triumph was a small collection of false-fronted buildings facing a dry, mournful main street where clumps of sage and sumac grew ignored. The dying sun glinted on the greasy glass windows of the two buildings that possessed them. The few people on the street glanced up without seeming interested as the party rolled into town.

'There you go,' Dallas said, pointing toward the first of the buildings they passed, The green wooden structure had the word 'Hotel' lettered across its façade in paint so faded that it could barely be read. 'Civilization, Carroll.'

'Pull up in front of it,' Cougar instructed Dr White, and the weary doctor, like an automaton, nodded and did so without discussion, the wagon creaking to a halt.

Cougar looked at the trail-tried Ellen White, grateful that she would at least have a bed to sleep in for this night. Weariness dulled the sparkle in her eyes. Her dust-streaked face and straggling hair attested to the heat of the day, the difficult miles they had traveled.

He expected to see her smile with relief. Instead, with the help of Cougar's hand, she simply stepped down to stare up and down the dismal street where here and there a lantern had been lighted already.

'You'll be safe for tonight, and a lot more comfortable,' Cougar said, trying to cheer her. 'They'll have a bathtub and we can find something to eat that wasn't cooked over a smoky camp-fire.'

'Yes,' she answered weakly, and she did attempt a smile of gratitude.

Cougar smiled in return. He was watching her closely, wondering. Their trek would only grow more difficult now that they had moved out on to the desert. They were in Indian country now, a land nearly waterless. Could Ellen endure the hardship to come? Even at Fort Apache the days would be searing and dusty this time of year. Her only company would be Mrs Crook and perhaps a few other senior officers' wives. There would be no shopping except for scarce and poor goods at the sutler's store, no chance of leaving the stockade to ride and explore the countryside without an armed guard. The food would be bad and repetitious — there would be no fresh fruit or vegetables, but only beef and beans with possibly a few supplemental eggs for day after endless day. Her quarters would be rough. Sand would blow in through chinks in the log walls and the air would be stifling. More than one woman had been known to go mad in this country. And more than one man.

'This is hers,' White said, handing a carpetbag down to Cougar as the doctor himself looped the reins around the brake handle. White took his own satchel and clambered down clumsily from the wagon bench, his muscles stiff from the day's sitting.

'I'll come back and see that the team's put up properly,' Cougar assured him.

'Yes, thank you,' the doctor said distractedly.

'I'll take care of the stock, if you like, Cougar,' Dallas said. 'I think that's a livery up ahead there with the lantern hanging out.'

'All right, Dallas. I'll be along shortly to give you a hand,' Cougar promised. Then he went to the tailgate and assisted D'Arcy from the wagon. Supporting Calvin's weight on one shoulder he led the way into the dark, dilapidated hotel.

A couple stood behind the counter, eagerly waiting for them. She was big and blowsy with a mop of tangled gray-blonde hair; he was narrow and balding beside her.

'Welcome to Triumph,' the man said in a reedy voice as dry as the desert beyond.

'Good evening,' Cougar said, tipping back his hat. D'Arcy braced himself against the counter, drawing the big woman's vaguely fearful eye. 'We'll need a room for the young lady here, and two doubles for the men. OK, Doc? It's best if you share with D'Arcy in case he needs something.'

'All right,' Dr White said. He muttered, 'Though there's not much left that I can do for him.'

The owner of the hotel registered them with satisfaction; paying customers were probably very few and far between way out here. Maybe he and his wife had hung all their hopes on making a success of it, betting Triumph would grow and prosper one day. From what Cougar had seen, it was a flimsy hope.

The little man showed them down a

corridor by lantern light. Ellen's bath was arranged for, although she looked like she would be flopped down on her bed sound asleep from exhaustion before they brought the tub and heated the water.

'Where's a decent place we could grab a bite to eat later?' Cougar asked.

'There's a restaurant right across the street,' the hotel man told him. It's called Cloris's.' He opened a window in Cougar's room with some difficulty to let the dry fresh air enter to wash out some of the dry stale air that now filled it.

Cougar tossed his gear on to one of the beds and started out again to help Dallas McGee with the stabling up of the horses. D'Arcy fell in behind him as he started up the hallway. Cougar stopped, shaking his head.

'Where do you think you're going, son?' Cougar asked him.

'I,' D'Arcy said definitely, deliberately spacing out his words, 'am going to find a beer!'

Cougar laughed. 'All right, Calvin. We'll catch up with you. Stay out of trouble.'

'I wasn't planning on dancing or fighting,' D'Arcy said. 'Besides, this town looks too poor to be able to afford trouble.'

Once outside Cougar watched his friend wander off up the street toward a low, lighted building. D'Arcy's arm dangled uselessly at his side and he moved clumsily. Cougar shook his head again with worried sorrow. Then, after pausing for a couple of riders to pass by, he crossed the street to the stable where Dallas McGee already had things well in hand. Cougar rubbed down his own two horses, and, checking to see if the stable had oats, ordered some for each of the animals.

Finished with that chore, the two former scouts left the stable to stand in front of the building, watching the long sky redden above the roofline of Triumph.

'What now?' Dallas asked with a yawn.

'D'Arcy went looking for a beer. I say we join him.'

There was no argument from McGee and so they sauntered in the direction Calvin D'Arcy had taken. The evening breeze had lifted a little and had cooled some, turning the evening almost pleasant. It didn't take much looking to find Calvin D'Arcy in that-sized town. He was sheltered in a low-beamed, squared-log building along the street, seated in a red-painted chair in the farthest corner. Three or four men, none of them talking to each other, had spaced themselves along a puncheon bar. The bartender wasted his time dusting off his stock. Cougar and D'Arcy bought a pitcher of beer and went across the packed-earth floor to where D'Arcy had already made a good start on his first drink.

For a time they contented themselves with sipping the warm beer, cooling down, enjoying sitting somewhere besides on their saddles.

The saloon was far from cheerful, but there was a pleasant, sheltered feeling about it as the three of them sat there in near silence. The room was like some hidden-away nook, dark and protected. Cougar liked the feeling. He might have been some primitive hunter fresh from a struggle with club-wielding foes, resting in the relative comfort and security of a safe cave dwelling. He realized, too, that they were all glad to be away from Dr White, whose ramblings had gotten more annoying and less oriented.

And beyond those feelings, he realized that already, somehow, he missed Ellen.

'Dammit all!' a voice bellowed out almost simultaneously with the banging of the saloon's door. 'Now, there's three of a kind!'

Cougar was facing the door and recognized the newcomer first — a scruffy man wearing dark jeans out at one knee and an underwear shirt crossed by suspenders. His head reminded Cougar of a turkey's head. Just now it was topped by a torn flop hat with an eagle feather thrust into the band.

'Skeeter Hicks!' Cougar called back. Dallas turned his own head, grinned, and waved the man over to their table. Skeeter moved with a noticeable limp, and after shaking hands all around with a grimy, horny hand, he sat down carefully, placing his stiff left leg out in front of him.

'What in the world is this?' Hicks asked as he looked from one face to the other and slapped his hand against the tabletop in glee. 'I never thought to see you three together again. And here?'

'How are you doing, Skeeter?' Cougar asked. He gestured to the saloon keeper to bring another glass.

'Doin'? Keeping body and soul together — almost, that is. I been doin' some smithin' and a little saddlework. But you three! General Crook must be in serious trouble if the army's scraping the bottom of this barrel.'

Which was very close to the truth, Cougar thought. Pouring each of them another beer, he asked, 'Is there any word floating around as to where the general might be bivouacked, Skeeter?'

'Nope.' Skeeter Hicks tilted his hat back so far that it looked like it would slide off his white-haired head. He lit a pipe, waved out the match, and said, 'There's not a whisper of that drifting around. If I had to guess I'd say that he's probably up in the Whites, chasing after Fox Ring.'

'Fox Ring?' Dallas said, taking a swallow of beer. His eyes narrowed with puzzlement. 'I never heard of him, I don't think.'

'You will,' Skeeter promised him. 'The farther west you ride, you'll damn sure hear plenty about Fox Ring. He's some cousin of Geronimo's, or anyway some kind of relative. They say he's cutting up pretty bad.' Skeeter frowned. He lowered his voice and looked directly at Cougar before saying, 'I hear that Quiet Star is riding with him.'

'What has that got to do with anything?' Cougar asked. He had felt his heart tighten just a bit but he wouldn't let it show in his eyes.

Skeeter met Cougar's eyes with his own, then broke off his gaze. 'I recall when she really had a case on you, Carroll.'

'That was a long time ago,' Cougar said. 'She was just a kid.'

'Sure she was.' Skeeter stretched and leaned back in his chair, shifting his stiff leg carefully. He continued to study the three men across the table in amazement. Long ago Skeeter Hicks had been a blacksmith for Crook and part-time handyman for the ladies at the fort, hanging curtains, papering their walls and such. He had fallen from a roof and broken his leg in two places. The army did nothing to help him but set his leg and inform him that he would have to be replaced, an event Skeeter was never bitter about. At the time he had said, 'They never promised me no pension. All they promised me was a

168

day's pay for a day's work. I kept my part of the bargain; they kept theirs.'

'Have you seen many Mexicans around, Skeeter?' D'Arcy asked, and Skeeter's eyes narrowed as he glanced now at D'Arcy's dangling arm. Obviously it was injured, but Skeeter didn't feel it was his place to pry. He answered:

'Now that's a mighty funny question, Calvin, this close to the border.'

'It might be,' D'Arcy agreed, 'but it might be important to us.'

Skeeter said, 'No more than usual, I don't suppose.' His eyes became cunning. 'But you're not talking about the local folks or the casual drifters, are you? You'd be asking about a body of armed men.'

'That's right.'

'I haven't seen a bunch like that. Just the locals, a couple of vaqueros trailing through from time to time. The usual crowd. Why, was you looking for them?'

'Just wondering,' D'Arcy answered, staring into his beer mug.

'Why, you three have become damned secretive, do you know that? All right,' he inquired, looking from one man to the next, 'what is going on that I don't know about?'

'Maybe nothing,' Cougar answered for the group. 'Anyway, it's nothing for you to worry on.'

'Meaning,' Skeeter said with a hint of bitterness, 'that it ain't none of my business.'

'Meaning,' Cougar responded, 'have another beer,' and he proceeded to pour him one.

'I have seen some strangers around here, though,' Skeeter volunteered after a sip. Foam flecked his upper lip and he licked it off. 'If it's of any interest to you.'

'It could be,' Cougar said cautiously. 'What sort of men? What did they look like, Skeeter?'

'Like nothin' in particular,' the old man said, 'except they was riding good horses, real good horses, and carrying a lot of guns. I don't think any one of them was wearing but a single belt gun. Every saddle had two rifle scabbards swinging from it. There was maybe six of them, Cougar. Looked like they'd ridden a long way. They just came into town, stocked up on supplies, and rode out again.'

'When was this?' Dallas asked with curiosity.

'Them? That was just this morning,' Skeeter told them. 'Do you mind if I take a little more beer out of that pitcher?'

'Finish it off,' Cougar said. He was glancing at D'Arcy and Dallas McGee; they were all thinking the same thing. The men Skeeter had described could have been those who were tracking them. It could have been anyone, of course; cowhands returning from a long drive, for instance. But the timing of their arrival and the number of men — six, as they had estimated — made it seem to be more than coincidence.

Apparently they had not given up on hunting them down, but simply pulled back temporarily for reasons of their own.

Leaving, Cougar paid the bartender and sent another pitcher of beer over to Skeeter. The three of them went out onto the buckled plankwalk in front of the saloon and stood in silence for a time beneath the sparkling desert sky. They looked the street over carefully, their eyes going to the end of the street and to the heads of the alleys they would be passing. Then, one at a time, they crossed to the hotel.

Ellen was in the lobby, seated on a faded red velvet settee. She had bathed and put on a clean white dress with lace at the cuffs and the neck. She wore a scent like lilacs. She seemed a lot better now, eyes bright, her hair pinned up, her lips smiling in greeting.

'What have you boys been up to?' she scolded playfully. 'Getting into trouble, I wouldn't be surprised to learn.'

'Naw,' Dallas drawled. 'Those dance-hall girls weren't no trouble at all, were they, boys?'

'None,' D'Arcy agreed with a smile.

'I'm really hungry after all that waiting,' Ellen said. 'You three must be starved as well. Shall we get Father and go out to dinner?'

'I'll get him,' Dallas volunteered. 'Whyn't you help me, D'Arcy?'

D'Arcy caught the one-eyed scout's wink and he nodded, glancing at Ellen and Cougar. 'Why, sure,' he agreed.

'You two might as well start on over,' Dallas suggested.

'But — ' Ellen started to object, but then she caught their intention, the amusement in their eyes. Smiling gratefully, she replied, 'That's a good idea. We'll find a table for all of us. Thank you Calvin, Dallas.'

She took Cougar's proffered arm then and they went out of the hotel on to the street. The night had grown soft and pretty, the stars blinking in the velvety desert sky. Ellen breathed in the cooling air deeply as Cougar guided her toward the restaurant across the street.

'That was nice of them,' she said,

looking up at Cougar so that some of the starlight danced in her eyes.

'They'll do, those two,' Cougar said. If Ellen noticed the way Cougar's eyes continued to move, searching the shadows and doorways, she said nothing.

The restaurant offered steaks and potatoes with biscuits and gravy. They ordered and were served coffee while they waited. The others were delayed: perhaps White was taking his own sweet time dressing; perhaps Dallas and Calvin were deliberately delaying the doctor so that Ellen and Cougar could have just a little time alone.

Ellen looked around the room, which was roughly constructed but clean. Steam warmed the interior of the restaurant and she could smell biscuits baking. She began to make some trivial remark when she noticed the intense way the scout's gray-green eyes were fixed on her. Surprised at the intensity of his look, she placed her coffee cup down on its saucer, cocked her head and asked him, 'Something's bothering you. What is it, Cougar?'

'I want you to tell me now, Ellen.'

'Tell you . . . ?' She shook her head with incomprehension. 'Tell you what?'

'About this,' Cougar said, holding up his arm to show her the woven silver and gold bracelet on his wrist. 'I want to know who the man was that was wearing it and why he came looking to kill.'

10

Ellen's mouth twitched nervously and she turned her eyes downward. When she lifted them again Cougar could see thoughts scrambling around behind them as she thought how to answer the unexpected question.

'All right,' Ellen said hesitantly, licking her lips. 'I was hoping we wouldn't have to talk about it at all — that you wouldn't find out. It's simple. The oldest of motives: they want the money.'

Cougar's heavy eyebrows drew together. 'Who wants the money? And what money do you mean? You said it was simple to understand. Make it simple for me.'

'The Brotherhood,' she said at length and Cougar's incomprehension only deepened. What in hell was the little woman in the white dress telling him?

'That's who it was.' She touched the bracelet on Cougar's wrist. 'They all wear one of those.'

'The Brotherhood,' he repeated. 'And just who might they be, Ellen?'

She turned her empty coffee cup nervously in her hands and glanced toward the restaurant door where none of their party had yet appeared. 'Father really wouldn't want me discussing this with you,' she said.

'I need to know, Ellen. If there's trouble following us, we have the right to know what's happening, how great the risk might be.'

'I know that,' she said very quietly. Then, determinedly, she told him. She began hesitantly and then spoke with a torrent of words now that the flood-gates had been opened. There must have been a lot of pressure building up in Ellen, a vow to be silent offset by a need to share her knowledge. She told Carroll Cougar:

'Back in St Louis where we had the church, Father had a body of 'saints' around him. That was what he called them, 'the Brotherhood of Saints'. They were like church elders, his apostles you might say. He promised them a lot . . . but they didn't get quite as much as they expected.'

'Such as?' Cougar asked, not unkindly. The girl was flushed and very nervous. He tried to soothe her with a gentle smile.

She paused again and shrugged, banishing obligations, then continued. 'I suppose it all started when something went wrong as Father was raising Luke Anderson from the dead!'

'When he was *what*?' Cougar shook his head as if his hearing had suddenly gone bad on him.

'When . . . when he was raising Luke Anderson from the dead,' Ellen repeated in a small voice.

Cougar asked patiently, 'What went wrong?'

'It . . . ' the girl was miserable. 'It didn't work,' she said.

'That I can believe.' What kind of

charlatan — or madman — was Dr White? 'So what happened next? No. Let me guess. The Brotherhood got mad about it.'

'Don't laugh at me, Carroll. I hurt too much to be laughed at. 'You're right, of course. They felt betrayed . . . and of course they were angry about the money they had donated for Father's new temple.'

'What went wrong with that?' Cougar asked, sighing inwardly, feeling deep sympathy for this woman who had been forced to endure such absurdity, and undoubtedly made to believe — or at least pretend to believe — in her father through all of this.

'There wasn't *time* to build it!' Ellen said, looking at him earnestly, leaning forward, small hands clasped together. Impatiently, she waved away an approaching waitress with a fresh pot of coffee. 'Everyone in the Brotherhood was suddenly so angry.'

'So they wanted their money back after the . . . mistake with Luke

Anderson. That's understandable to me, Ellen.'

'No!' she objected. 'Don't you see, it wasn't fair. Father couldn't give them back their money, because then how would the temple ever be built? And it must be, you can see that,' she said to a dazed Carroll Cougar. He could only nod, indicating he was still paying attention.

'What did your father do with the money?' he had to ask.

'It's under the wagonbed floorboards. It's Father's, isn't it! After all, those people gave it to him freely to build the temple. What right do they have to get it back?' Her question was weakly indignant.

'I think you know the answer to that, Ellen.' Impulsively, he took her small hand in his large, callused one and she burst into tears. She shook her head mournfully.

'Oh, Carroll, it was so awful. They threatened us and saw to it that Father couldn't practice medicine anymore.

No one ever came to his office and the Brotherhood destroyed our property at night, taunting us as we tried to sleep. I was frightened out of my mind. We had to slip out of town in the dead of night.'

'All right,' Cougar said softly. 'That part is all over and done with now. You're with us; it'll be all right.' Would it? Cougar was angry and it showed, no matter how he tried to conceal it from a hopeful Ellen. Damn all! Hadn't it ever occurred to White what his machinations had done to his daughter? She had tried her best to be loyal and found herself the victim of deceit. Hadn't White paused to realize that his actions could even have gotten Ellen killed?

The only sensible solution, of course, was to give the money back, but apparently White would have none of that. He must have it to build his temple where he could commune with spirits and raise the dead. Cougar had asked himself earlier if White was a charlatan or a madman — now he thought he had his answer.

Cougar meant to have a very serious talk with the man, and if need be, he would tear that wagon apart and find the money himself if it would keep Ellen safe and relieve her of her burden. The next time one of the Brotherhood men showed up, he was welcome to the money. He, D'Arcy, and Dallas had enough trouble without having this piled on top of it. It was nearly time for Cougar to part company with all of them anyway, as much as he would miss Ellen. Now wasn't the time to tell her, but he meant to be going it alone soon.

They were getting very close to Alamo Banks, the last place Solon Reineke had been seen. It was nearly time to find Carlina's killer.

Nearly time to go tracking.

* * *

Dinner was a slow affair. The food was plentiful and good, but there was little conversation. No one was in high spirits. White spent his time glowering at Cougar. Seeing Ellen's blush, her averted eyes, the minister somehow knew that she had broken down and told Cougar something, if not everything. White ate in silence and scowled at the scout. Perhaps that was meant as a cautionary expression. He might have suspected that Cougar had pumped his unworldly daughter and gotten her to reveal the presence of the stolen money. Frankly, Cougar didn't care except for the discomfort it obviously caused Ellen.

When Cougar had seen Ellen to her room he went to his own room and passed through to the balcony where he leaned against the wall, arms folded, thinking deeply. When he had made up his mind he turned and re-entered the room. Dallas had come in behind him and was seated on the edge of one of the beds, tugging his boots off.

'Go fetch D'Arcy, will you?' Cougar asked, and with a puzzled look, Dallas padded off in stockinged feet to do just that.

When the three men were together in the room with the door closed, Cougar told D'Arcy and Dallas McGee, 'I'm pulling out come dawn.'

'So soon?' D'Arcy said in surprise.

'It's time,' Cougar said with finality. Then he explained to them about the group of men called the Brotherhood while they listened first with amusement and then with real concern.

'That dumb bastard, White,' D'Arcy muttered savagely.

'Is that who those six men are?' Dallas asked.

'Who knows? If they are then we've still got three other trackers to account for. I'm just telling you so that you'll know. The last thing you need is another risk.'

'Damn right we don't,' D'Arcy said heatedly. 'I'll tear up the wagon myself.'

'And do what with the money?' Dallas asked quietly.

'You're right,' D'Arcy admitted grudgingly. 'What then?'

'What do you suggest, Cougar?'

'We could leave a note here addressed to the Brotherhood. If any of them comes looking for us, the clerk could give them the note. Tell them that if they send a single unarmed man up to you you'll break out the money and turn it over.'

'No good,' Dallas thought. 'How would we know that it's the rightful owners? If we just hand the loot over to anyone who might come across the note, the real Brotherhood could show up later — and then we wouldn't have the money to turn over to them. It could make them just a little peeved.'

'Well, as for the note,' Cougar told them, 'we won't mention money, of course. We'll say that we have some goods belonging to the church. No outsider is likely to consider following after you on the chance of grabbing a box of Bibles.'

'No, I guess not.'

'As for being positive that they're the right people, Ellen will recognize any man from the Brotherhood,' Cougar pointed out. 'Besides,' he said, holding out his wrist to remove the bracelet that he now gave to D'Arcy, 'whoever comes, he'll be wearing one of these.'

'All right,' D'Arcy said with resignation, slipping the bracelet on his own wrist. 'I guess it's the best plan we can come up with. I haven't got any other ideas.'

'We could just ride out and leave White on his own,' D'Arcy said. 'It'd serve him right.'

Each of them looked at D'Arcy's withering arm and knew that he wasn't going to be riding anywhere. Neither Cougar nor Dallas mentioned that, however.

'Well, he wouldn't be exactly alone. He'll have Ellen with him a lot of miles from any law. We can't leave her.'

'No, we can't.' Dallas rubbed at his bad eye and then raised his hands, palms up in a gesture of resignation. 'We'll have to do it your way, it seems, Cougar. Good luck. We'll see you in General Crook's camp.'

'Sure,' Cougar said, but his voice wasn't all that confident. They all knew what still lay ahead. The trouble hadn't even started yet.

★　★　★

In the morning Cougar dressed, picked up his worn saddle, and went out, closing the door silently. He paused in front of Ellen's door for just a moment and then clamped his jaw and went out into the gray of pre-dawn. When the first streamers of color began to touch the eastern sky, he rode out on the buckskin horse, leading the sorrel, which carried his small pack. From the window two men watched him until he had disappeared, then, turning from it, Dallas spoke to D'Arcy.

'You're never going to tell him the truth about Solon Reineke, are you?'

'No.' D'Arcy lifted an eyebrow. 'Are you?'

'It's not my place to do so,' Dallas answered. Then he turned back toward the window for a silent moment before he belted on his Colt and went down to breakfast.

Despite missing Ellen White, the feeling of freedom rose up through Cougar like a fresh inner breeze. He was where he belonged — alone on the broad, sunrise-colored land with a good horse between his knees and a good rifle in his hand. Doves rose from their nesting places and cut quick silhouettes against the painted sky as they flew toward water. A coyote, startled as it sat in the shade of a scrubby mesquite, a dead cottontail at its feet, picked up the rabbit and loped away before the horse's hoofs could bring the man-thing nearer. In the distance the mountains picked up the first rays of sunrise and their tips glowed golden while their flanks still hid shyly in purple shadow. The ocotillo had begun to bloom and their crimson flowers, perched atop their long, whip-like stems, flanked Cougar's trail.

There were men riding behind him

half a mile or so, but he would worry about them later.

For now he rode steadily on, onto the desert flats, letting the buckskin canter smoothly over the broken ground, the sun at his back, Solon Reineke ahead of him.

It wasn't much of a way to look at things, to live, Cougar considered as he rode. All of his thoughts were fixed on the past with Carlina or on the future he must face with Reineke. It was as if he did not live much now. Even back on his little ranch he had not truly been happy. Chores, a book, an occasional trip to town or a visit with a neighbor occupied his time; yet those around him had homes, children. Laughter rang in their throats when they were amused. Cougar knew he was stunted in some ways by his brooding. People considered him a morose, solitary bear of a man. Maybe that was all he was now. Maybe that was all his future was to hold if he could not exorcise his personal demons. But he was incapable of forgetting Carlina; not able to forgive or forget Reineke's crime.

Cougar had not always been that way. He used to laugh a lot himself; now it seemed he barely smiled. Would killing Reineke bring back the old Cougar or only make his life darker yet? Now he rode alone, nearly fearlessly, across the Indian-infested, dangerous land, and he knew where his fearlessness had its roots — a man has to have something in his life he refused to let go of to fear death. An empty man is a fearless one.

There was Ellen, of course ... He paused for a moment to let his mind focus on her almost fragile appearance and contrasting inner strength. There was Ellen, but he knew he was not the man for her even if she would have him. He could not draw her down into his dismal world. No. Let her go to balls with clever young army officers, or with a well-groomed businessman with money in the bank and prospects ahead of him ...

The first shot whipped past Cougar's ear as he crossed the dry wash, and he flung himself from the buckskin's back as three more shots followed in rapid order. He scrambled to his feet and dove into the dry brush along the wash. The sorrel reared up and broke away from its tether. The buckskin, calmer, stood looking around in confusion. Bullets sent up sprays of sand and pebbles in Cougar's wake as he darted for another, deeper stand of gray willow and sumac brush, cocking the Spencer .56 as he wove his way through the tangle of undergrowth.

He had lost his hat and low, lying on his belly, he wiped his sandy hair away from his eyes and looked out toward the low knoll to the south where the shots had come from.

'Idiot,' he said, scolding himself. Daydreaming in a country like this, knowing there were hunters all around.

He crabbed his way a little to his left where the sandy ridge in front of him was higher, forming a slightly better barricade. Then he waited.

The sun was drifting higher; the sand grew hot beneath his body. A stream of red ants trickled across his trigger hand. Cougar heard a small sound, but it might have been the breeze, intermittent and hotter now, shifting the iron-gray brush surrounding him.

Maybe the snipers had pulled out already, trying a few quick shots on the off chance that they would score, then withdrawn to try again at a better ambush spot farther down the trail. Maybe . . .

Two more closely spaced shots ripped into the white sand in front of Cougar and he ducked his head as pebbles and sand splashed into his face. He thought he could see a distant curl of rising smoke as he lifted his eyes, but it was nothing to shoot at.

Opposite him was a low mound with scattered mesquite and desert sage. He believed that this was where the shots now had their origin, but he saw no movement, no inexplicable bits of color or shadow. Nothing at all.

Another shot rang out and this one scorched the flesh on the pad of Cougar's left hand. A slow rivulet of blood began to trickle from the shallow wound down his wrist.

That was too damned close. They had him pinned down good and proper, and whoever was shooting had an eye for it. He didn't fire back this time either, although he spotted some gun-smoke for sure after the last shot. Even knowing their position, there wasn't a lot of sense in shooting at smoke just to let them know that he had teeth. They certainly were aware of that already. They were cautious in the manner of men who knew their work. Cautious and patient, and that was the way a tracking man got things done.

Cougar looked around carefully, keeping his head low. The wash he had allowed himself to be trapped in remained at its present depth of three or four feet for about fifty yards north and south, but to the north it eventually began to deepen and appeared to fork.

Two more shots were fired, not as close as the earlier one. In the back of Cougar's mind knowledge stirred. For the last few minutes only one rifle had been firing, keeping him pinned down behind his sandy bunker. Earlier there had been at least two rifles firing. He was sure of that. Without noting it consciously at the time he remembered now having heard the sharp crack of a Henry or a Winchester and then the heavier boom of a buffalo gun, maybe a Spencer .50. All right, then; where in hell was the second rifleman?

The only answer was that he was trying to set up a crossfire, somehow flanking Cougar, but then Cougar had seen no movement out on the desert. No one crossing the arroyo.

Two more rifle shots bored in too close for comfort, making Cougar's mind up for him. He was liable to be killed by sheer accident if this went on. He would have to move. So long as he remained where he was, it was only a matter of time before they got him, and they had all day to get it done.

Cougar's mouth was dry, his eyes gritty from the sand they had caught. Again he looked northward up the gully. It would have to be that way. He would have to try moving to where the sides of the wash rose higher and a running man could move in a crouch, avoiding detection. There was no chance at all of reaching his horse — the buckskin that still stood thirty yards away on the flat, aimlessly tugging at a clump of dry buffalo grass. Of the sorrel there was no sign.

There was no choice but to move, and so he moved.

Sliding back a little from the protective ridge, he began to belly down toward the wash over hot sand and rocks. He crawled as rapidly as possible, rifle across the crooks of his elbows. If they charged him at that moment, he was a dead man, he knew. He scuttled forward, his chin inches above the ground, tearing elbows and knees on the rocks of the dry streambed. The earth became nearly bald; nothing grew there but a few clumps of greasewood, useless for cover.

Still there were no more shots. Shadow stretched out and touched him. The wash was growing deeper. Cougar lifted himself cautiously into a crouch, panting now as he looked toward the sandy knoll where the sniper was positioned. By now the man would know that he had moved — if he was still up there — and it wouldn't take a genius to deduce which direction he had taken.

The wash, as he had believed, did fork off here. To the west it became shallower again. He could not go much farther than fifty yards along it before it petered out. To his right, to the east, the wash deepened still more. There was some greasewood there and scattered willow brush with one bedraggled, dead sycamore still rooted to the dry earth. Gnats swarmed around Cougar's face and a deer fly bit his neck painfully.

He made up his mind and moved into the deeper wash even though it was nearer to the snipers' position and down there he could not rise up to peer over its banks, which were all of ten feet high.

Jogging now, he followed its twisted course over uneven ground and rocks deposited there by flash floods. Sweat stained his shirt at armpits and throat. His feet burned.

The floor of the arroyo rose again as he followed a turn it had cut. He was now no more than five feet below the rim of the bluff and he eased forward in a crouch. Panting, Cougar pressed himself to the bank of the gully and looked carefully over the rim. Looking back toward the knoll he could now see a horse, indistinct and dark, but no sign of a rider.

A whooshing sound behind Cougar caused him to spin around. He put his back against the bluff and brought his Spencer up as an Apache warrior on horseback gave a whoop and leaped his pony into the gully from the opposite rim.

Cougar fired as the horse's shadow cut out the sunlight. His bullet went up along the side of the pony's neck and exploded the Apache's face. The horse rolled headlong into the gully, throwing its dead rider. Cougar lunged to one side to avoid the tumbling body of the over eager warrior's paint pony.

When he again scrambled to his feet the pony was upright, racing down the gully, hind legs kicking out with the frustration of pain. A second Apache had rushed up and launched himself from the bank toward the big man. Both men fired their weapons while the Apache was airborne, and both men missed their target as the warrior tumbled to the ground at Cougar's feet. The Indian was up quickly with his Yellow Boy carbine in his hands, fire in his black eyes.

Cougar swung out savagely with the muzzle of his Spencer and metal clanged on metal as he slammed the

Indian's carbine from his hands.

The Apache was quick, stocky, his face murderously dark. He had a long-bladed knife in his hand already and before Cougar could fire his rifle the Indian had leaped at Cougar, slashing down at the scout's chest.

Thrusting his rifle out with both hands to block the downward cut of the knife, Cougar threw himself on to his back against the sand. As he landed, he kicked out hard, flipping the lunging Indian over his head but losing his Spencer in the process.

Cougar drew his bowie knife and came to his feet at the same time as the white-clad Apache. The two men's eyes locked briefly in savage challenge and they circled warily before the Indian launched himself at Cougar again. Carroll managed to sidestep the Apache's charge and throw out a boot, which tripped the warrior.

The Apache landed on his face against the sandy bottom of the arroyo, but managed to roll to one side before

Cougar, throwing himself at his fallen enemy, could finish him. Cougar landed awkwardly, grappling with the Indian. The two men locked hands, clawing at each other's wrists. The Indian writhed, spat, and cursed in his own tongue, striking out wildly to try to dislodge Cougar's grip, but it was to no avail. Cougar had fifty pounds on the brave and was by far the stronger.

The wild look in the Indian's eyes already reflected a knowledge of coming defeat as Cougar slowly, relentlessly forced the Apache's free hand down, the bowie in his own grip following until it plunged into carotid, the rising blood gushing from the Indian's throat, spraying both of their heated bodies.

Still the Apache struggled and twisted and Cougar stood pressed against him, holding the warrior's knife hand pressed to his thigh until there was no more movement, until the brave's heart had stopped beating and the rawhide-handled knife fell from his hand to glitter against the hot desert sand.

Slowly, clumsily, Cougar disentangled himself from the Apache and let him slump to the earth. Cougar's heart was pounding wildly. His breathing was raspy and labored.

Then, recovering his rifle, dusting it off, he stood looking down at the two dead Indians. They were both very young. Their war had begun early, he thought.

And it had ended early.

Moving with extreme caution, he worked his way back toward his horses. The land was utterly still in the moments after death. No other men moved on the wasteland. It was a good bet that his pursuers had seen the Apaches and pulled off to a safe distance. A single buzzard soared overhead. Soon there would be more of them.

He managed to approach and gather up his buckskin horse's reins without bringing gunfire on himself. He swung heavily into the saddle, putting his recovered cavalry hat back on his head. The dry desert wind whipped the perspiration from his body. The blood on his shirt and hands had dried to a crusty deep maroon. He collected the sorrel, which approached him carefully, perhaps wanting to know if the man-trouble was now ended. There was no sign of the Indian's paint pony. Perhaps the bullet had struck more deeply than Cougar had thought. He preferred to think that it had tossed its hackamore and run off to rejoin some mustang herd.

In the distance now as he started the buckskin forward, he could see the silver thread of the Blue River and the thrust of the Mogollons. There lay the town of Alamo Banks. There the trail began. For it was there that Solon Reineke had last been observed. With luck Cougar would reach the town by sundown.

He rode slowly on, moving like a shadow through the rising heat veils.

Carefully as he rode, he reloaded his rifle and wiped it clean with his scarf. He would have other uses for it in the days to come.

11

Alamo Banks was a fair-sized town for this part of the desert. As its name indicated it was situated on the bank of a tributary of the Blue River surrounded by cottonwood trees. A plank bridge a hundred feet long crossed the river and led Cougar into the town as sunset again began to paint colored images across the pale skies and the sun rushed toward the shelter of the distant mountains.

There were six saloons, a hardware store and an emporium, a hotel, dance hall, gunsmith, hostelry, feed store, and a smith's shop among other hopeful endeavors, built in even rows spoking out from the four corners on Main Street. The streets were sand and much of the town was coated with alkali dust. The scent of river was pleasant in the hour of dusk. Drifting from uptown somewhere came another even more pleasant scent, that of pies baking, and Cougar's stomach tightened a little in response.

The shadows, already long, merged and pooled rapidly as the brief desert twilight colored the hills and the sand desert to the west with a pinkish hue. Wearily, Cougar swung down from the buckskin as he reached the stable. He put his horses up, untying his pack from the sorrel, leaving his saddle and spare rifle in the care of the stablehand. The night was splendid as he stepped outside of the musty barn. It was still, the first star blinking through a sheer veil of color above the darkly silhouetted mountains. An owl hooted from the cottonwood grove beyond the town.

He was weary, but there was an excitement in him. He was at the head of the trail. He would find Solon Reineke and put the man down. Not only would he be helping his country by stopping the traitor, but he would be giving himself a deep, long-withheld satisfaction. Nevertheless there was a certain sadness riding with him, a loneliness. He had left Ellen White behind. True, she had two good men to watch out for her, but would she wonder why he had left her? Likely, he thought. How could she understand even if he had explained it?

Still, he couldn't completely banish her memory and his concern for her. 'Where are you tonight, girl?' he asked the unresponding night. Then, with some anger at himself in him, he shuffled down the dusty street toward his lodgings.

*　　*　　*

She looked skyward in time to see the falling star arc toward the dark, jagged mountains. She murmured something and then sighed. Ellen was just outside the ring of light the campfire cast, needing to be alone in the evening coolness for a time after sitting in the hot sun all day with only the creaking of the wagon wheels, the bobbing of the horses' heads, the endless expanse of the desert, and her father's occasional loud 'Hosannas'.

'Are you all right, Miss White?' D'Arcy asked. He was so near that she started at first. All of these scouts, wilderness men, moved so silently that it was unnerving at times being around them.

'Yes,' she replied in a voice that was slightly shaky. She turned toward him, her hand at her throat. 'Thank you, D'Arcy.'

'I was just a little worried about not seeing you. Cougar would want me to keep a close eye on you.'

'Would he? D'Arcy — why did he have to go?'

'You know why, miss; he went hunting.'

'But why did he have to ... ?' She waved her hands in frustration. 'Oh, it's just that I miss having him around.'

'Yeah, I know.' He put a comforting

hand on her shoulder and Ellen jerked away, even knowing that Calvin D'Arcy meant nothing by it. His hand dropped slowly to his side. 'Cougar — he just does what he thinks needs to be done and there's no talking him out of it once he's decided for himself what he thinks is right.'

'No matter the cost,' she said numbly.

'Just about,' D'Arcy was forced to agree. 'Like I say, that's Carroll Cougar for you.'

'You've known him a long time, haven't you, D'Arcy?'

'About seven years, I'd guess,' D'Arcy answered. They had started walking back toward the fire together.

'Has he always been like this?' she wanted to know.

'Like what? A warrior, do you mean?'

Ellen stopped and turned to face D'Arcy.

'No. I mean has he always been so . . . gruff,' she said, groping for a word to convey what she meant.

'I don't know,' D'Arcy answered. 'He's not really so gruff. He's a big laughing man sometimes . . . or was.'

'Was? That might be so. I've certainly never heard him laugh since I've met him. Why is that so, D'Arcy? Is it me? Us? What changed him? You must have been there.'

D'Arcy looked at her in thoughtful silence, then he shook his head. 'I guess he'll tell you himself someday,' he finally answered. 'It's not for me to say. Goodnight, miss,' he added, and then he turned and walked away from her, leaving her more confused and frustrated than ever.

'Jawing with the lady?' Dallas asked, looking up from where he sat on his saddle, poking at the low fire with a stick.

'Sort of. I was just checking up on her to see if she was all right.'

'You'd better watch yourself, D'Arcy,' Dallas McGee said with a crooked half-smile.

'Don't worry about anything like

that,' D'Arcy replied, his voice indicating that he saw no humor in the remark. He squatted down, hooked the coffee pot from the edge of the fire, and poured some into his blue tin cup.

'Do you ever think about the money the doctor's supposed to have stashed in that wagon?' Dallas asked. This time he did not look up as he asked the question. He sat on his worn saddle staring at the fire. The flickering light from it cast a strange, impenetrable gleam over D'Arcy's one good eye.

''Course I think about it! That's a damn fool question, Dallas. We've got to have it ready in case those Brotherhood men show up, don't we?'

'That's not what I mean,' Dallas said.

'What *do* you mean, then?' D'Arcy asked cautiously.

'I mean this — like, that's just wild money, isn't it? It's no one's really. Hell, D'Arcy, why am I trekking this desert to go back and see if I can get myself killed with General Crook this time around? Because I'm broke, that's why.

Hell, I'm more than broke, Calvin. I owe some people money — a lot of money — from that land company scheme of mine that fizzled.'

'I hope you're not suggesting what I think you're suggesting,' D'Arcy said.

'Me?' the one-eyed man said as if in surprise. 'All I asked was do you ever think about the money, Calvin, nothing more. Because I think about money. Almost all the time.'

'I'll tell you what, Dallas — I wouldn't do so much thinking about that money,' D'Arcy said to his old friend. 'Or if you do, think about it this way — suppose that money came up missing. Then suppose the Brotherhood decided to take their anger out on Ellen. Then suppose Carroll Cougar heard of it. Suppose you was gone because you had taken off with some money. You got to get a hold on your supposing, Dallas.'

Dallas McGee was silent for a second or two, then he grinned. 'Yeah,' he said as he rose, tossing his stick into the fire.

'I see what you're telling me. I guess when a man gets to thinking about money, he'd best think it all the way through.'

Then he nodded goodnight and drifted off toward his bedroll, his boot heels sending up puffs of dust. D'Arcy watched him go and then, with a shake of his head, finished his coffee and kicked out the fire, wandering toward his night-watch position on a low, sandy knoll beyond the wagon.

Ellen removed her boots and slipped into her own bed beneath the tailgate of the wagon. The fire was a softly dying glow; the stars were growing brighter. A coyote howled out on the desert and was answered. There was a following cacophonous yapping of her pups and the world went silent again until sometime later Ellen's father spoke from his own bed inside the wagon.

'Ellen,' he hissed, 'can you hear me?'

'Yes,' she said softly, sorry to have her own distant-dreaming thoughts inter-rupted.

'It's all clear to me now, dear,' Dr White said.

'Is it?' she asked around a yawn. She knew that things always came suddenly clear to her father at this time of the night — although nothing clear ever really resulted from these sudden inspirations of his. She waited patiently for him to explain this night's epiphany.

'I was meditating,' White said, his voice insistent, fervent. 'And it came to me quite clearly, Ellen. It's all quite simple, really.'

'Yes?' she responded, yawning again.

'It's the Indians, you see.'

Her eyes came wide open suddenly and she stared upward to where her father slept. 'What Indians? What do you mean, Father?'

'I contacted the spirits . . . it's all clear now. It's so obvious. I was a fool not to realize before why I have been sent out here.'

She felt a chill over her flesh like icy fingers. *What now?* she thought, and anguish closed her eyes and forced a single tear from each of them. It was so hard to trust in her father's dreams at times, to try being faithful as a daughter should.

'I am meant to go among the Indians,' Dr White said. His voice was a rapid, excited whisper. 'It is they who will welcome me. It is among the heathen that I shall build my temple!'

Despite the near terror in her heart, the anguish she felt for her deluded father, Ellen nearly burst out laughing. She forced herself to say in measured tones, 'I am not sure they would welcome you, Father.'

'Of course they would!' he said irritably. 'You just don't understand, Ellen.' His tone was now that of one lecturing a child. 'There are certain things you will never be able to understand because you haven't yet made the necessary spiritual connection — or tried that hard to do so, I am forced to add.'

'Father,' Ellen said, growing worried that this was not just a fanciful whim.

'The Indians are at war with us. They are very likely to hurt you, you have to realize that. They will not listen to your teachings, believe me.'

'You do not possess strong faith, Ellen,' White said, scolding her but sounding weary at the same time. 'My own daughter! Haven't I taught you well? We must follow the wishes of the spirits, you know that.'

'I think it is time for me to go to sleep now, Father,' Ellen said, deeply troubled now. 'Perhaps I am too tired to follow your thinking. Maybe in the morning my mind will be more alert.' Oh God! she was thinking. Had he finally reached the last outpost of sanity, this brilliant, educated man?

'You mean that you think it is time for *me* to go to sleep.' White said in an angry whisper. 'I see now that you will never truly understand. You can't even envision the temple of gold, the Indians flocking to it, entering their own salvation. I must be missionary to them! Someone must save them from themselves and it is I whom the spirits have chosen.'

Ellen found that she was trembling despite the warmth of her blankets. 'Explain it all to me again in the morning, Father,' she pled. 'Please! It is too late for me to understand right now.'

Then White was silent. She heard him turn over angrily in his bed, his body thumping against the bed of the wagon. She stared at the stars for a long while afterward, watching their slow progression. When she could no longer keep her trail-weary eyes open, she too rolled over and went to sleep, but not before murmuring, 'Oh, Cougar! Where are you?'

She seemed to sleep for ever in some blue-white desert dream-land where robed figures trod by. Cougar was there but he was far distant and did not speak. He was too busy with his own affair — spinning a stone wheel that seemed to do nothing at all except send up fountains of sparks . . .

Then Ellen was awakened to the shouts, the squeal, the blizzard of dust, brilliant sunlight in her eyes and the mad cracking of a bullwhip. There was no reality to it as she passed from a deep, confused sleep to sudden, disordered awareness. She couldn't untangle herself from her blankets, and when she did she looked across the camp to see D'Arcy sitting up in his morning bed, and Dallas McGee scrambling down from the dune where he had taken over the night watch before dawn.

The wagon was gone!

By the time Ellen got to her feet, she could see only a portion of it far out on the desert flats, dust feathering up from its wheels, canvas flapping. D'Arcy, panting with excitement, was beside her now and she gripped his arm.

'They pulled it right off over you!'

'Father!' Ellen said, looking around wildly. 'He's gone.'

'He sure as hell is,' Dallas said, arriving with his rifle in his hand, his single eye glowering. 'He's the one driving. I saw him. What was I supposed to do? Stop a man from hitching his own horses?'

'Why would he . . . did he say anything to you, Ellen?' D'Arcy asked.

'That doesn't matter,' she answered, her entire body shaking with terror. 'You've got to catch him. Stop him!'

'The horses are scattered,' D'Arcy said. He was still bootless, his eyes clogged with sleep. 'Someone cut 'em loose and shooed 'em off. I looked.'

'You have to go get them, round them up!' Ellen shouted frantically. 'You have to follow Father before he — ' Then she clenched her jaw and said no more. The two men looked at each other.

'Dallas?' D'Arcy asked.

'Well, of course we got to find our ponies, but they could be a mile away. There's no hurry about it that I can see — the doctor's going to be long gone before we can catch up our stock and saddle them. Besides,' he added, 'I'm not likely to be following him the

218

direction he's taken. He's heading right into the heart of Fox Ring's renegade territory.'

'But you must!' Ellen insisted. 'D'Arcy — surely you will.'

'Miss,' D'Arcy said with a heavy shake of his head, 'what I must do is reach General Crook with some information I have. It's far more important than trailing after your father at the moment. I'm sorry, but that's the way it is.'

'She spread her hands helplessly. 'You just can't let him go off alone like this.'

'We can, miss,' D'Arcy answered, not without compassion for the girl; but the damn fool, White, had made his own decision to do what he was doing, whatever the reason. 'We can because we got no choice, miss. I have a duty to others. Dallas,' he said to the one-eyed man, 'let's round those horses up.' Ellen White was left to stand alone on the empty desert, watching the now barely visible dust her father's wagon trailed behind it drift up into the blue-white morning sky.

★   ★   ★

The door to the saloon banged open and the big man in the buckskin shirt and old cavalry hat burst through it. He walked to the bar, not bothering to close the door although the winds were pushing desert sand through into the interior of the gloomy building. The bright rectangle of light seemed to offend one of the patrons and he kicked the door shut; Carroll Cougar wasn't even aware of it. His cat eyes, gray-green and glaring, were fixed on the man behind the bar.

He was massive, bigger than Cougar even. He wore a shabby, once-white apron over jeans and a red-checked shirt. His chest was a bear's, his eyes were sullen and held the look of a man who has seen much trouble come and go and who has taken care of all of it with the confidence of cruelty. His fists, often broken, were twice the size of an ordinary man's, his arms as solid and well-carved as any made from oak could have been. He didn't welcome the stranger kindly. The look in Cougar's eyes was also unmistakable. He was a stalking man; there was no doubt about it.

'Get your ass out of here, stranger,' the bartender said, reaching beneath the bar where his ten-gauge greener with the sawed-off barrel rested.

Cougar, trudging steadily toward him, never stopped. The bartender flinched, taking half a step back, and Cougar, grabbing him by his shirt front, sent a right hand crashing into the man's face. Then agilely, swiftly, he was across the bar, bringing the side of his hand down against the bartender's wrist, cracking bone there, and the bartender dropped the shotgun with a howl.

The bartender threw a wild punch at Cougar, but the scout just shifted his feet a little and the fist bounced off his shoulder. Still moving forward, Cougar marched the man in his grip lengthwise behind the bar, glasses and bottles toppling to the floor.

'Where's Reineke?' Cougar demanded.

The bartender's back came up against the wall and again he threw a desperate punch, which Cougar blocked before answering with an overhand right of his own that split the bartender's cheek open.

'Where's Reineke?' Cougar repeated. He held the bleeding bartender against the wall with one hand around his throat.

'I don't know what you mean,' the bartender answered in a strangled tone. He was still surly, belligerent. 'I don't know what the hell you're talking about.'

Cougar hit him again. This one slammed into his gut, doubling him up. As the bartender gasped for air, Cougar demanded again, 'Where's Reineke? I know he was staying in the back room here. I know you and he were whiskey-and-cards buddies.'

'Go to hell . . . ' the bartender, his face blanched, his eyes watering, spat back. He was a tough cookie, indeed. Cougar hit him again, starting blood flowing from his nose. The soft voice from behind Cougar spoke.

'You don't have to go through all of that, mister.'

Still propping the bartender up, Cougar turned his head slightly to see an older man in a faded blue suit, black hat pushed back off his forehead, studying him.

'I'll tell you which way he went. No need beating up Morey here.'

Cougar gave the bartender a last, shoving lick for good luck, walked around the bar as the eyes of the motionless man who had spoken to him stood there watching.

'You know something about Reineke?' he asked the man in the blue suit.

'I know he offered to kill me one night. I know I'd have killed him if I'd had the tools on me. He said I was bottom-dealing, which I wasn't, but he had lost a lot of money and was pretty drunk. The boys broke it up. Later on I saw him outside. He was talking to a fancy-dressed man, a foreign kind of gent wearing muttonchops. I pulled back into the shadows so he wouldn't see me and maybe start up again. I heard Reineke tell this gent that he was heading up toward Trampas Ranch. That's in the Gila Mountains. Reineke told this other gent that it was time to get things started. What things I have no idea.'

'That was all?' Cougar asked, one eye still on the bartender, who hadn't yet tried moving off the wall where Cougar had pinned him.

'That's all I heard. They split up then and left. I sure didn't follow after him, the mood he was in.'

'When was this?'

'Only a couple of days ago.'

'Where do I find this Trampas Ranch? Do you know where it is?'

'I can draw you a map.'

'Do it.'

'Now?' The man in the blue suit blinked at Cougar.

'Now.' Cougar put a gold eagle down on the bar and it was snatched up in a flash.

'You got it, mister.'

'This foreign-looking man — did he seem like he was going to ride with Reineke?' Cougar asked.

'I don't think so. He said something that sounded like he was 'going to the fort'. Something like that. The words weren't clear and he had some kind of accent anyway. I didn't catch it exactly.' The man scribbled out a map on the back of an envelope with the stub of a pencil. He looked at what he had drawn twice, shrugged and handed it over to Cougar. 'That's the best I can do. I hope it's worth ten dollars to you, mister.'

'It is.' Cougar lifted his eyes again to the bartender, who still held back hesitantly, blood trickling from his nostrils and split cheek. 'Here,' he said to Morey, 'for the mess. Buy all these boys a drink — keep what's left for yourself.' He slapped another ten-dollar gold piece on to the bar, inadvertently losing one of the Prussian gold pieces at the same time. It clinked to the floor and the man in the blue suit picked it up, squinted at it, and handed it back to Cougar.

'Now that sure is funny,' he said.

'What's that?'

'That foreign coin there,' he said, nodding at Cougar's palm. 'Reineke tried to spend one just like that by accident one night in here. I saw it plain as day. It had the same markings.'

Cougar made no reply. He turned and walked from the saloon.

He was saddled and mounted in fifteen minutes and with his canteens refilled was on the trail again. Trampas Ranch, was it? He did not know it, but if it was there, he would find it. He raised his gaze to the mountains.

He would damn sure find it.

12

'We got Apaches, D'Arcy,' Dallas McGee said, and the dark-eyed scout with the wounded arm looked behind them. He squinted against the brilliant morning sunlight and then managed to make them out. A small band of Apaches was following them. Five, maybe six warriors keeping well behind them, but on their trail.

'We sure do,' D'Arcy answered more calmly than he felt. He glanced at Ellen, who was mounted on the pinto pony Cougar had supplied to D'Arcy as a spare horse. The girl was pale, biting at her lower lip, afraid to look behind her.

'Don't you worry, miss,' D'Arcy said. 'They see three riders, armed, and they don't know one of them's a woman. Maybe they all got rifles, but more likely some of them have only bows and arrows or maybe lances. They know we're well armed or we wouldn't be riding out here. Two on one isn't good enough odds for them out in the open like this.'

No sooner had D'Arcy made that proclamation than the first shot rang out from the Indian band, followed rapidly by a dozen others. Looking back, Dallas could see the Apaches beginning a long charge across the flats.

'Ride, dammit!' Dallas yelled. 'D'Arcy, you never could out-think an Apache.'

They dug their heels into their horses' flanks and bent low over the withers, riding hell for it away from the Apache rifles. There was just no cover to be taken on the desert flats and there was no sense in halting to try having it out with the Indians there.

Ellen's heart hammered wildly. Although the guns aiming at them were distant, and with the Apache horses at a full gallop the bullets had little chance of scoring a hit, there was still that small chance. One of their horses could break its leg, she could fall from her mount, though her grip on the reins and pommel was fierce . . . anything could happen. She simply clung to her pinto and let it run as fast and far as it could, trying valiantly to keep up with the two men on their larger mounts. Cougar's sorrel had taken its own notion, flung off its lead rope and with D'Arcy's curse following it, galloped southward, deserting the party.

It was only a few minutes later, although it seemed like an eternity, that the Indian's shots faded to silence, but they rode on hard and fast, wanting as much distance as possible between themselves and the Indians. Their American horses, larger, better fed, had won their lives for them, far outpacing the stubby, range-fed mustangs the Apaches rode.

Finally, they slowed and D'Arcy, now coated with dust from face to feet, grabbed for his canteen and said,

'Young bucks, damn 'em!'

'What?' Ellen asked dryly, reaching for her own canteen. Her innards felt like they had been shaken to a new position. Her thighs and hands were sore.

'Just a bunch of kids, probably,' Dallas explained. 'Out raising hell, wanting to have some fun with us. No war party would have been so foolish as to attack us like that. They would have waited until dark, tracked us slow.'

'I hope they had their fun,' Ellen said bitterly. 'I was scared stiff.'

'Be grateful, miss,' D'Arcy told her. 'It could have been a hell of a lot worse than that.'

'Yes,' she said quietly, re-corking her canteen, 'I do realize that.'

And in D'Arcy's words, she realized, was the implicit prediction that it would get worse before this was over.

She felt genuine panic. Why was she so afraid now, when the trouble had passed? Why now did her limbs tremble and her heart continue to pound? She trusted these two men, but still she was deeply frightened even in their company. Why did she think that she wouldn't have been much afraid at all if Cougar were there?

They walked their tired horses on, plodding across the vast emptiness of the white-sand desert, none of them speaking. Ellen glanced briefly over her shoulder, looking to where the Apaches had been.

It was in their direction that her father had driven the wagon.

She turned her eyes forward again and rode silently on, the pinto now shuffling its feet as it plodded on beneath her. She patted the horse's sweaty neck, adjusted her hat and settled in again for a long, long ride across that bitter desert. She could only keep her spirits up at all by reminding herself that she was riding toward Cougar. If everything worked out she would see him again soon. She straightened in the saddle as more cheerful thoughts arrived to bolster her, and forced the weary pinto to lift its head and walk on.

* * *

It was dry and airless in the long red canyon that wound among the peaks and bluffs surrounding Carroll Cougar. Gnats and flies swarmed around his face and bit at the buckskin horse's eyes. The bottom of the canyon was mixed sand, rock, and red clay.

All through the afternoon he had seen no living thing but a lone jackrabbit and a snake or two. The silence when he halted his horse to measure the land was eerie in its completeness. Sweat stung his eyes and trickled down his spine.

At noon of that day he had crossed the narrow canyon floor, following a breakdown in the surrounding bluffs. Obviously, the crossing had been used in the past as a trail from one side of the small canyon to the other, and there for the first time he had come across the tracks of a lone horse.

Grass bent over by the passing of the horse had sprung up again in the impression of the hoofprints so the tracks were not fresh, but recent. How old? A day, perhaps, or two. But he had found a single rider moving where a lone rider would not usually ride in this time of peril. He could only hope and expect that it was Reineke.

He had marked the tracks well in his mind, noting that the left front shoe was chipped, the left rear built up, one nail missing. It was those tracks he now followed doggedly. Where they would lead him he did not know, but they were tending in the general direction of Trampas Ranch, according to the map that had been sketched for him.

At a feeder canyon the rider had veered off and headed upslope, moving though heavier brush over rocky ground toward the heights where a few wind-stunted pinyon pines grew. Cougar turned his horse's head that way himself, riding cautiously. There was no telling what surprises these hills might hold.

The canyon opened suddenly on to a small pocket valley, and although Cougar could cut no sign of the man he had been trailing entering it, he swung down toward it anyway, following instinct and logic. The valley was a pretty little place, half-surrounded by red hills dusted with yellow grass. It was as airless as the canyon floor below, however, and felt even hotter despite the greater altitude.

Ahead Cougar could see a break in the hills where there seemed to be a trail out of the valley. Midway to it, he came across an old fire ring on the slope. Tilting his hat back, Cougar looked around carefully and then swung from the saddle for a closer inspection.

The fire ring itself was big enough to indicate that a large number of men had camped there, and by working around it, looking carefully at the ash-coated earth, he was able to make out the signs of many men coming and going to the fire. How many it was impossible to say as each set of bootprints overlay the other. His guess was twenty, but it could have been twice that many. And they were not cowboys.

The bootprints were those of military boots with rounded toes, not those of a Western rider. Straightening up, Cougar frowned and looked toward the break in the hills. There was no true trail that he could make out, but the notch was certainly passable.

He walked on that way, leading his horse. He hadn't gotten far before he found the wagon-wheel tracks. And then another set of them. And a third.

Three wagons transporting men wearing military boots way out here? It was clear that the men were indeed riding in the wagons, not mounted, for outside of the team horses, Cougar could find only four other sets of horse tracks.

And one set of them belonged to the

horse he had been following since Alamo Banks, across the canyon to the campsite.

Back there was a pool next to the south bank, watered by a seep above — undoubtedly one reason the party had stopped to camp there. Was another reason to wait for the lone rider that Cougar had been tracking?

Squatting down next to the notch in the bluff as he studied the tracks, he split a blade of grass with his thumbnail and watched thoughtfully as his own horse grazed.

'Reineke.'

He said it with conviction. He had believed that was the man he had been tracking since Alamo Banks, of course, but now some intuition made Cougar certain of it. It had to be. What townsman would wander this devious trail and meet a group of soldiers in the hidden valley? It was Reineke, meeting a group of soldiers to act as their guide. They were not American soldiers, for they were not cavalry. The army did not send foot soldiers out on to the desert.

He thought now of Trampas Ranch. Was he already on it, or was that ahead somewhere over the notch's crest? Was it to be a sort of staging area for the coming assault on American troops by the mingled force of Indians, Mexicans, and Europeans? Cougar shook his head, not knowing, but feeling relatively certain in his own mind that this was indeed what was happening.

He walked to the buckskin and tightened the cinches on its Texas saddle again and mounted. 'Let's go find out,' he muttered, and he started on.

A six-point mule deer stood not a hundred feet from Cougar, just watching with unusual boldness as if he knew the man-thing did not dare fire his rifle. Not a mile on a large badger, even bolder, made a brief charge at Cougar's horse before it made its way away toward its burrow, still snarling and showing its savage little fangs.

There were flowers scattered across

the floor of the notch: owl's clover, and blue gentian. It was a place a man could enjoy wandering in another time, under other circumstances, Cougar thought, and that thought revived the painful memory of the plans he had once formed for his Twin Creek Ranch. Plans half-completed or forgotten. Things he had once wanted to do for himself, the right woman, and hopefully for their kids. The second well he had never got around to digging, the room he had never added on to the cabin . . .

None of that bore thinking about now; it seemed so very far away and long ago.

Not knowing what he was riding into, Cougar carried the Spencer .56 unsheathed. He considered the Winchester needle-gun, his spare with its 16-shot magazine, but he was comfortable with the Spencer and preferred the stopping power of the larger-caliber seven-shot carbine.

The crest of the notch was just above him now, a bluish doorway to the sky.

Cougar rode more cautiously as he neared it, keeping now as much as possible to the wall of the canyon. He found that his muscles had bunched involuntarily and he breathed in deeply, slowly, to relax himself.

Yet when he topped out the rise he was still alone in that tangle of hills and deep canyons. He saw no man, no animal, no structure across the hazy distances. Thunder rumbled to the north, surprising him. Looking that way he saw a column of cloud rising above the peaks. He sat his horse, one hand on the pommel, the other gripping the Spencer's receiver, just looking at the wide country below him.

There were only so many ways a loaded wagon could go to traverse the convoluted land. He unfolded the map the man in the saloon had drawn for him once more and compared it to what he saw. The envelope map wasn't elaborate, to be sure, but he could recognize much. There was no mistaking the big red mesas, twin sentinels ahead of him, or the jagged, broken ridge to the north. Somewhere between them, according to the sketchy map, lay Trampas Ranch.

Cougar rode on, leaning slightly from the saddle to more clearly see the line of the wagon tracks, which had faded as he crested the notch and met rockier ground. Lightning struck once far to the north, seemingly from clear skies, and thunder rumbled again. The gods were warring.

Darkness found him still on the trail. He achieved the highest ground possible, meaning to make his bed before it was totally black and the coming rain flooded the low-lying areas, and it was then as he reached the brushy hillrise he had selected, that he saw it in the distance: a light, bright and clear in that sunset hour.

Cougar tried to judge the distance and assess the route he would have to follow to reach the light — it had to be Trampas Ranch he saw. Then, making a sudden decision, he abandoned his plan of making a night camp and started on, the only illumination in the skies the occasional flash of lightning against the desert sky.

He let the horse pick its way for the most part, only guiding it in the general direction of the distant light, which had now divided and proven to be two separate light sources. One was obviously a camp fire — it was this larger light that Cougar had seen from the distance. The second glow was of low firelight glowing in the windows of a house.

The wind had begun to whip and wail in the canyons and the first raindrops now began to fall from out of the darkly boiling skies.

Cougar was too close to the ranch now to take any chances. He had found a clearly marked trail and now rode it warily. If these were hostile men as he believed them to be, there was every chance that a trail into the ranch would be guarded, as remote as Trampas Ranch was.

He made a decision to veer off the trail, taking his horse to higher ground, working his way carefully through the cold rain toward a ridge overlooking the lights. When he reached the crest of the low ridge he was astonished to find himself looking practically straight down on another structure with smoke rising lazily from its chimney to merge with the turmoil of the skies.

Cougar slipped from the saddle, tying his horse to a dead and stunted oak, which tilted southward, indicating the direction of the prevailing winds.

The building below him was of squared logs and very long, with few, small windows. Three iron pipes rose from the roof. It was obviously a bunkhouse. The other building, the one he had initially seen, was made of stone, two-storied and solid-looking. Around these two structures was a variety of outbuildings, a smith's shack, a smokehouse, a toolshed.

Farther away yet was the campfire Cougar had already spotted. The flames still glowed brightly in the gray of the falling rain, and by this wavering light Cougar could see three covered wagons, undoubtedly those he had been tracking since the teacup valley.

The bluff where he now sat his horse was steep and slippery but not so steep that it could not be negotiated on foot. Lightning flashed again across the tumultuous sky and, glancing that way automatically, Cougar cursed softly. For by the eerie light cast by the jagged stroke of lightning, he had seen a guard, rifle slung across his shoulder, standing watch farther along the ridge.

Not wanting to be seen himself, Cougar eased back toward where the buckskin horse was picketed. Untying it, he moved it back farther from the rim into a tiny, nearly hidden canyon mouth. Then he started back — for he had already made up his mind.

He was going down.

If Solon Reineke was on the ranch, Cougar was going to find him.

There was still some nagging doubt

in Cougar's mind that all was not as it seemed to be, that he might be making a vast mistake. There was even the possibility that he had been following the wrong trail since Alamo Banks, the possibility that the man who had drawn the map for him was lying, that Reineke hadn't been heading for Trampas Ranch at all, and that Cougar had been sent on a wild goose chase. All points that needed to be resolved and would be on this cold, rainy night. There was only one way to do that: go down and have a closer look.

Cougar looked to the unsettled skies and started back toward the bluff through the increasing rain to recover the buckskin.

He had nearly reached it when the guard stepped out from behind a boulder with his rifle lowered at Cougar's belly.

13

Cougar felt his heart stop and his blood grow cold. The guard had him good and proper. Even in the darkness he could see the grin on the sentry's face.

'Just where do you think you're going?' the guard asked, stepping nearer.

Cougar managed to sound indignant. 'Why, damn your eyes! You know exactly where I'm going. What in hell is the matter with you?'

The guard hesitated, fearing that he might have made a mistake. He stepped nearer to take a closer look at Cougar's face and Cougar's hand shot out, grabbing and lifting the rifle barrel. Simultaneously, Cougar stepped in and clubbed the guard to the ground with a smashing, right-hand blow.

The guard's eyes rolled in his head and he flopped backward on to the muddy ground, out cold. Cougar winged the sentry's rifle away and crouched down, binding the man's legs hastily with his own belt, tearing a sleeve from his shirt to tie his hands behind him, gagging him with his own bandanna. Then he rolled the guard into a clump of sumac and started on his way again.

The guard should have been tied up well enough so that he would not get free on his own, but there was a chance that he might somehow wriggle free and an even better chance that someone would notice he was missing from his post and go looking for him. Sooner or later a relief sentry would certainly arrive. That left Cougar without much time. There could be nothing leisurely about this expedition; he would have to get down there, spot his man if possible, and get the hell out of there fast.

The rain grew even more intense, the clouds had dropped very low. The flame of the sputtering camp fire glowed dully. Cougar could not hear a sound around him but the keening of the wind and the fall of the constant rain.

Half-scooting, he went down the fifty-foot bluff, moving toward the barracks, but keeping enough distance from it so that he could not be spotted by someone standing in the doorway idly watching the storm — or so he hoped.

He did not expect to find Solon Reineke in that bunkhouse, barracks, whatever it was. Reineke was the kingpin of this entire plan and he would likely be in the big stone house with whatever master planners there were around.

Rounding the yard to the back of the barracks Cougar remained in a crouch for long minutes, listening and watching the surrounding darkness. Now he could hear men's voices but they were muffled and indistinct beyond the log walls of the building.

Satisfied that all was quiet he moved on toward the stone house through a stand of large oaks. The shadows beneath them were nearly all-concealing, and when two men, joking and staggering, passed by him unaware of his presence as he stood next to the trunk of an oak only twenty feet from their path, he shivered with relief. He couldn't expect to repeat the luck he had had with the guard on the bluff.

He knew there would be men guarding the stone house as well, and was hardly surprised when a flicker of sputtering lightning illuminated two of them together in front of the building, standing dismal duty in the rain. Cougar watched them for a full ten minutes, getting their patrol pattern down.

At intervals one of them would call to the other and make a circuit of the house, calling out again as he returned. All of it must have seemed ridiculous to the two who knew how far from civilization they were and assumed that no enemy could even know of their existence.

Their generals were more knowing. They were on a perilous mission, seeking to grab a portion of territory from a powerful foe. In time of war there was no such thing as having too much security, especially not around the general headquarters building, which, in effect, was what the stone house was.

Biding his time impatiently, Cougar watched through the rain. He now began to work his way toward one end of the building where he crouched, waiting for his man to call out and begin his circuit of the house.

When he did, Cougar moved quickly.

He raced toward the shrubbery at the side of the house, reaching it before the guard had regained his post. He knew exactly how much time he had before the other guard made his circuit and he used it to lift himself up to peer into the rain-smeared window above him.

That window provided no information. It was a bedroom with a lamp burning low on a carved bureau, totally empty just then. That meant he would have to try to circle to the other side of the house to look inside. Getting there would be trickier, but knowing the guards' routine he thought it could be done.

He crouched in the damp, thorny shrubbery again, waiting. He heard the second guard call out, and Cougar drew himself more deeply into the shrubs as he waited for that man to pass him in the direction opposite to that taken by the first. Slowly, with palpable boredom, the guard slogged past Cougar's position just a few minutes later.

When the guard had rounded the corner of the house, Cougar moved again, slipping toward the back of the house to the windows there. Again he chinned himself on the sill and this time his efforts were rewarded.

A dozen or so men sat inside a sort of library or stood beside the big stone fireplace, drinking brandy from snifters, smoking cigars. Some of the men wore uniforms, some civilian clothes. The uniforms were like none Cougar had seen before.

One of the men in civilian clothes crouched rather than stood near the fireplace. He smoked a cigar intently, dark eyes smoldering like the tip of his cheroot. He was an Indian — that was immediately apparent — uncomfortable in the clothes he wore, uncomfortable in his surroundings, unsure of his company.

Cougar knew without ever having seen the man before that this was Fox Ring, the Apache leader who had made a pact with the whites to wage war against the United States.

There was a red-faced man with silver hair, and a popinjay of a man in uniform complete with braid and fringed epaulets, a row of medals on his chest and a gentlemanly-looking Mexican with carefully barbered hair and long, graceful hands. Their heads turned in unison at some sound Cougar could not detect from beyond the window and the red-faced man grinned. A newcomer entered the room. He was tall, wearing a black suit, his thinning hair slicked back over a narrow skull. He held a drink in his gold-ringed hand. It was Solon Reineke.

It was all Cougar could do to hold himself back. To prevent himself from firing through the window, killing Reineke then and there. But he wasn't feeling suicidal on that night.

One of the guards shouted from the front of the house and with a low curse, Cougar dropped away from the window. He should have had the time to take his look and slip away again, but he didn't. Something — who knew what instinct — had prompted the sentry to hurry his routine and Cougar found himself face to face with the man as he rounded the corner of the stone house.

Cougar brought his fist up in a violent uppercut, clacking the guard's teeth together, snapping the man's head back. Dropping his rifle into the mud, the guard fell backward.

Looking around anxiously, Cougar rapidly dragged the guard into the bushes, stripped off the man's coat and hat and put them on. Returning to the sentry's position he yelled out as he had heard them do half a dozen times, 'Clear!' Then he waited.

Had it not been for the rain and the dark of night he would have already been discovered. As it was it was chancy enough. He stood in the drifting rain, muscles tensed, eyes alert, fighting the instinct to make a run for it. After an interval that seemed eternal the second guard called out, 'Walking!' and began his own circuit.

Cougar had seen all that he could hope to see on this gray night and so he started toward the oak grove. He would have no more than a minute before the alarm was raised and he had fifty men on his heels.

Cougar sped through the oaks, weaving his way. He was panting with the exertion; the cold rain streamed into his face. His clothing was soaked through, heavy and damp. He was approaching the end of the barracks, still at a dead run, when the cry went up from the porch of the stone house. It takes a minute or two for anyone to respond even to peril, and Cougar was already scrambling up the muddy bluff in the darkness before the barracks door was flung open and men swarmed toward the stone house.

Rapidly, Cougar clambered up the dark, sodden bluff, wanting to get to his horse and get the hell out of there. If no one had come across the sentry he had tied up in the meantime, he should be able to make it, for no one was yet spreading out to search for the interloper. Reach the horse. Find sanctuary. Then figure out a plan for getting to Reineke. He had at least located Solon, and that was a start.

Cougar didn't slow as he passed, but he saw the struggling guard he had tied earlier still lying in the brush. Cougar grinned despite his dark mood. They would find the sentry soon and outside of some embarrassment the man hadn't suffered any real injury.

The rain continued to sheet down, masking the mouth of the small canyon where he had left his horse, but Cougar found it, and still jogging, went to the waiting buckskin. Once into the saddle, he would be gone into the night-shrouded hills and the army below wouldn't have a prayer of finding him.

Cougar had yanked the buckskin's tether free and had grabbed the pommel to swing aboard when he heard the ratcheting of a hammer behind him.

'Don't,' a voice warned as he started to crouch and reach for his Colt. 'It's your own Spencer I'm holding. I thought you'd have quit carrying it a long time ago.'

Slowly Cougar turned, his hands level with his waist. He found himself looking right into the muzzle of the big .56. The woman holding it was perched almost lazily on a rock as the rain swept down. Cougar knew her immediately.

'Hello, Quiet Star,' Cougar said to the Apache girl.

'Hello, Cougar. What madness are you attempting now?'

'Just roaming.'

'Yes. Always roaming. I'm surprised you recognized me,' she said, sliding down from the granite ledge to face him, the rifle barrel still raised.

'You look the same.'

'I was just a girl when you knew me,' she said.

'Yes,' he said, 'just a girl.' But still he had recognized her instantly. She was more mature now, a little fuller of figure with a tighter, or perhaps wiser, look in her doe eyes.

'I did not ever thank you for the last time,' she said, stepping still nearer, but not dangerously so.

'You wanted to get away from the reservation; you got away,' Cougar replied.

'Twice before that you are the one who took me back, however. The third

time I escaped,' Quiet Star remembered.

'You got lucky,' the big man said.

'I saw your eyes go past me, Cougar,'
she said with just a hint of a smile. 'I
was hiding in the brush beside the river.
I saw you following my tracks and my
heart beat frantically. I would not go
back! But they had sent Cougar again.
How could I hide my tracks from
Cougar? I had done everything I knew.
I traveled up and down in the river's
water. I leaped from rock to rock,
walked backwards and erased my tracks
from the sand with a length of brush. I
did all I knew how to do but when I
saw Cougar following after me, I knew
I had failed again to escape.'

'I guess you did not fail. If I recall I
lost your sign along the river. I can't
remember now, all those years ago,'
Cougar said.

'I remember,' Quiet Star said, 'and so
do you. I watched you come nearer and
nearer. I saw your eyes go past me as I
lay trembling. Then I saw you ride on,

still looking at the ground as if you were hunting for my tracks, but you were not. You let me go.'

'Maybe,' he admitted.

'I know you did. I know you had decided to let me be free.' Her eyes widened with delight as she saw the object hanging at the V of his shirt. 'You still wear that!' she exclaimed. Quiet Star lowered the Spencer now, stepped forward and touched the silver disc he wore around his neck. 'It is only a child's thing, made with a girl's unskilled hands.'

'Yeah,' Cougar agreed. 'I can still wear it, can't I?'

'Yes.' The delight faded quickly and then she stepped away, looking into his eyes. She held the rifle tightly still, but not menacingly.

'What are you doing here, Cougar?' she asked in a whisper he could barely hear above the rain. Her eyes were very wide, childlike themselves now with curiosity.

'Maybe tracking you, Quiet Star,'

Cougar answered with a grin.

'This is no time for laughter, Cougar. It is a dangerous place you are riding, very dangerous.'

'That was Fox Ring I saw down at the house, wasn't it?'

'How did you . . . ? Yes, it was Fox Ring.'

'Making war talk.'

Quiet Star started to lie to him, but there was no point in it. Cougar knew or he wouldn't be here. 'Yes.'

'Why weren't you down there?' he asked. She was all but concealed briefly by low, scudding black clouds. Thunder rumbled in the mouth of the canyon to the north.

'They did not want me there,' she replied, 'and I did not wish to be there. That is simple to understand. When he learns what we must do, Fox Ring will tell me.'

'You know, Quiet Star, that it is you who are now traveling a dangerous trail, not me. You know that, don't you?'

'There is no path left for the Apache

that is not dangerous,' she answered sharply. 'Not any longer.'

'This will be worse than any you've ridden,' Cougar told her seriously.

'No.' The girl in the mist shook her head deliberately. 'This will succeed. Fox Ring is certain of that, Cougar.'

'And if it doesn't succeed?'

'It will,' she said almost desperately. 'You do not know what strength we have now.'

More reflectively, she added, 'And if it does not, at least we will have made the good fight. We will have done all that we could for our children and our grandchildren to save their land and our way for them.'

'You have to listen, Quiet Star; it will never work. You can't whip General Crook.'

'Crook . . . ' She almost gave away something that she believed Cougar did not know — that Crook would be dead before the war even started. 'Crook can be beaten,' she said with confidence. 'Any warrior can be beaten.'

'Maybe,' Cougar said. He did not want to argue with the young woman; he believed he understood her thoughts. Anyway, there was nothing he could say to change them and he hadn't the time for a long discussion. 'I've got to go now,' he said. 'If they catch up with me, it won't be pleasant.'

'No.' There was the briefest hesitation, a moment when Cougar considered that Quiet Star, no matter their past, might hold him for the searchers below, but then she nodded and handed him his rifle and he swung aboard the patient buckskin horse.

'I guess I won't be seeing you again,' Cougar said. He removed his crumpled cavalry hat from his saddle-bags and jammed it on to his head. The rain continued to intensify. Quiet Star answered through the steel mesh of the rainstorm.

'No. Cougar,' she said imploringly, 'be wise and ride far away from this. Don't look back.' Quiet Star pleaded with him. She placed her hand on his saddle skirt and looked up at him with proud eyes that nevertheless revealed concern. The time they had shared together — girlish dreams, foolish chatter — were long gone. The time of caring for Cougar had passed.

'I can't ride away for the same reason you can't, Quiet Star. It's my battle too, now. Men have come to me and asked me for my help. I can't turn my back on them. It has nothing to do with what I think or feel. It has to do with duty.' Through the rain he asked one last question: 'Fox Ring — is he . . . ?'

'He is my husband, Cougar. He is a good, strong husband.'

'Take care of him, then. Get him out of his territory. Go across the border to Mexico. You'll be safe down there.'

'My husband has his duty as well, Cougar. You should understand that. Besides,' she said with a sort of weariness, 'Crook would follow us there, no matter what the laws are. I know this.'

'Maybe,' Cougar admitted. 'Quiet

Star . . . what were you doing up here by my horse? Out in the darkness and the rain?'

'The guard did not come in to be fed when it was his turn,' she answered. 'I found this horse. I was waiting to find the white man who owned it. And kill him.' She handed his rifle to him solemnly, and he took it.

Cougar made no reply. Distantly, he heard a muffled yell and then another. He touched the brim of his hat and turned the buckskin toward the main canyon, vanishing into the night and the storm as the Apache woman watched his back, remembering a different time and long-ago friendship before she, too, left the little canyon and hurried back toward the ranch where the angry search for Cougar had begun.

14

Night-time found the three riders camped on a small rocky knoll dotted with catclaw and agave. One huge live oak inexplicably flourished there, its wide-spreading roots presumably finding water where none could be seen to exist. Ellen was more tired than she could ever remember being. She was a good rider, but an entire day in the saddle virtually without rest was too much for her. Her back ached, her legs felt raw and sore. At sunset she stood alone in the purpling evening, hands on her hip, staring back in the direction they had come from. She still hoped that somehow her father would see his mistake, turn around, and catch up with them.

She still couldn't decide if she was more worried for him or angry with him. It was a fool's journey he had undertaken.

All of her clothes save those she was wearing were on the wagon; her soap, hairbrush, everything she needed and owned. Distant thunder caused her to turn her head. There was a storm in the foothills, but Dallas and D'Arcy said they expected it to continue eastward and not reach them on the flats. Too bad, she thought as she wiped her dusty hands together. After a day beneath the firebrand of the desert sun, she would welcome a thorough drenching, a flood!

She turned and walked back to where the two men sat close to the small fire burning bright against the dusky light, drinking coffee. Dallas glanced up at her approach.

'Are you all right, miss?' he asked, studying her face.

'I'm just tired, that's all.'

'You have the right.' Dallas nodded in response.

D'Arcy offered her a cup of coffee which she took absently. Her thoughts had drifted to her other lost man, to Carroll Cougar. Where was he on this night? She leaned her back against the oak, watching a flight of nightbirds far out across the desert.

'We should make Fort Apache by tomorrow,' she heard D'Arcy say.

'And just what will I do there?' Ellen asked with an edge to her words.

D'Arcy and Dallas exchanged glances. That question had already occurred to both of them. With her father's surgeon's position, she would have had security, even if the life out here in this raw land would be tough on her. Now, with no father to provide for her, what *would* she do?

Ellen snatched up her single blanket and turned away from them. She leaned up against the base of the tree, her head back, her eyes closed. *What would she do?* Her hopes for building a new life for her father and for herself had become a nightmare. She sipped indifferently at her coffee and continued to sit and stare at the darkening

266

desert, finding nothing attractive in its changing hues, long valleys, and distant, bulking mesas.

Where are you, Cougar?

'Did you want to take first watch?' D'Arcy asked the one-eyed man.

'Sure. I'll take it, Calvin,' Dallas said. 'I've got some spark left in me still.'

'You're doing better than I am,' D'Arcy replied. Despite the breeze from the desert flats he was perspiring freely. Fresh blood soaked his chest and arm. It was obvious that his wounds were on the verge of destroying him. Instead of mentioning this he told Dallas, 'It's gonna be tough on the lady, even should we get through to the fort.'

'It will, for sure. Even if the Indians don't burn it down or we abandon it if open war breaks out, I don't know what kind of work she could get. Laundry, maybe,' he said doubtfully.

With that in mind, perhaps, D'Arcy said, 'I wonder how Cougar's getting along.'

'Hell, you know Cougar — he's all right.'

'Maybe. He sure walked into a hornets' nest, though. Of his own accord, too. He's not seeing straight these days, thinking of getting Solon.'

'Cougar takes care of himself. I'd rather be in his shoes than Reineke's. Hell,' Dallas pointed out, 'you've put yourself into a devilish position as well. Trying to get to Crook through all these hostiles, not even knowing where he's camped.'

'And you, Dallas?' D'Arcy asked. At Dallas's puzzled expression, D'Arcy pointed out to the one-eyed man, 'You know as much about everything now as I do. They've got just as much reason to kill you as they do me.'

'Yeah,' Dallas said quietly, his eye meeting D'Arcy's across the dully glowing, dying camp fire. 'It does give a man pause to reflect, don't it?'

D'Arcy didn't answer. He was on his feet, catlike, instantly. Dallas whirled, drew his pistol, and crouched beside him. 'Did you hear it too?' he whispered.

'Yes, I did. But what . . . ?'

The question was never completed. Abruptly, from out of the darkness a howl rose into the night and something was thrown toward them across the camp and into the coals of the fire. D'Arcy and Dallas both looked for targets for their guns, but could sort out nothing in the darkness beyond the camp's perimeter.

'Are they gone?' Dallas asked in a taut whisper after several long minutes of waiting.

'I think so.'

'Apaches, do you think?'

'I'd say so. But what in hell . . . ?'

Now Ellen White screamed beside them as they continued to study the deep desert shadows by starlight. She had rushed to the fire, her blanket over her shoulders. Now the blanket had fallen away. Frowning, D'Arcy and Dallas strode to the fire ring.

'Damn all!' D'Arcy murmured, for

now they could see clearly what it was that the Apaches had thrown at them: the head of Dr White lay smoldering in the coals. Staring up blankly at them.

D'Arcy turned the girl away. She screamed again and then shrank in his arms, shaking uncontrollably. Dallas stood staring down at the gruesome object. 'Damn all!' he said softly, and then he toed it from the coals and pushed it off into the underbrush. It was then that the girl screamed again.

And again.

It was not long after that that the storm drifting in from the hills to the north reached them and the rain began to fall.

* * *

Cougar was already soaked through. He was on a low, folded hill, watching the men below him search intently for him, an impossible task under these conditions. The searchers had been given what was essentially an exercise in futility, poking around in the dark and rain, undoubtedly cursing and grumbling at their miserable task, but someone had wanted Cougar badly enough to send them out searching.

Now and then he could hear fragments of speech. Once he saw a man light a match, cup it in his hands and crouch down. The tiny flame illuminated the resentment on his face at having been dragged from a warm bunk to pursue this unlikely task. The searchers managed to draw no nearer to Cougar's position.

Any tracks he had left had long ago washed away or been crisscrossed many times by their own boots. Cougar reflected that he could have rolled up in his blankets and slept safely for the past few hours while the men below wasted their time. So long as he cleared out of the area before daylight, he had no real problem. The skies above the dark land parted just long enough for a hesitant silver moon to peer briefly through the tumbling clouds and Cougar watched it as it was rapidly swallowed again by the continuing storm.

Cougar took his time, thinking things through methodically before he made his next move. He had found his man — Solon Reineke — but just how was he going to get his hands on the killer? It was possible, he considered, to lay in wait and snipe the man, but Cougar didn't want it to be that way when the time came for the killing to be done. He wanted Reineke to see him face to face, wanted him to know that it was Cougar who had found him, Cougar who was going to take his life as Reineke had taken Carlina's life.

For now he could only sit brooding, the rain curtaining off his cavalry hat, the reins to the buckskin in hand as the hunters scoured the muddy, broken land for his sign.

He thought briefly of Ellen White, hoping she was all right, sure that she was in good hands. He didn't really know what to make of that woman. One thing was certain; there could never be anything between them. She was too much the lady and he just had nothing to offer. Besides that, he knew with certainty that thoughts of Carlina would always haunt his house — and that was painful and unfair to any woman, trying to compete with a ghost who could forever forward do no wrong.

Cougar heard a low whistle and turned his head. Squinting into the darkness and rain he saw two mounted men working their way slowly toward the position where he now rested. Now just what was it they thought they had found? He hadn't come that way. No matter; if they continued the way they were coming they would eventually find him.

They dipped their horses into a brushy draw and rode up the near side, riding directly toward where Cougar watched and waited. Still Cougar did not move, not believing that the two could possibly know they had him. Obviously, however, he couldn't delay withdrawal much longer without his movements being seen.

Scowling, he stood and walked the buckskin back a little away from the rim. It was time that he had to be moving, but which way? He knew he still had searchers on the far side of the hills where it broke off into the little valley. That meant his best move was to go upslope. He lifted his eyes toward the brow of the low mesa. Long, stark, he believed he could make out a sort of natural ramp sloping toward its heights.

Maybe, maybe so. There wasn't any time to hesitate and debate the plan. The hunters on horseback were much nearer now. He could hear the chinking of their bridle chains. Cougar swung aboard the buckskin and started away, working his way through the maze of boulders and scattered oaks toward the mesa while the cold rain continued to fall.

The moon again broke briefly through the shifting clouds, lighting his way with a faint, silvery glow not much brighter than starlight. He kept to the concealment of the rocks and trees even though it was slow going, until he reached the foot of the ramp he had seen. He checked it again from this distance and now was fairly sure he could ride up it to rimrock despite the steepness of the incline. The buckskin was a mountain horse and good at picking its way.

The moon still shone, but thunder boomed near at hand, rumbling across the forlorn valley. Cougar heeled the buckskin and the horse started up the long, rock-strewn grade.

It was forty minutes or so, no longer, when Cougar lifted the buckskin up and over the mesa lip on to rimrock. There he swung down, patting the buckskin's neck, loosening its cinches as he let the animal blow. The storm had shifted southward now, breaking up somewhat, and now by moonlight Cougar could see out across the valley floor far below. The riders trying to cut his sign had lost his trail — if they had ever actually had it, and he could see them distantly, riding in the opposite direction, following a gully, which now ran with a narrow white-water surge.

'Now, just how do we get down again?' he asked the buckskin, which pricked its ears curiously. Cougar patted its flank, tightened his cinches again and swung aboard, crossing the mesa by the eerie light of the moon playing among the ragged, silver-edged clouds.

He was into their camp and among them before he even saw them and the four men surrounding him rose from the ground with their rifles in their hands, their sights on Cougar.

'Where you come from, mister?' one of them, a man with a long thin beard, asked.

Cougar took a slow, deep breath and casually swung down from the saddle, holding his free hand high.

'I didn't mean to come up on you boys,' Cougar said as innocently as he could. 'But you had no fire — well, that's good. I like to be among cautious men.' He already believed that he knew who it was he had run into, and there was just no choice but to stall. He wasn't going to try shooting it out with four armed men who had the drop on him. He had to run his bluff, and it had to be a good one.

Another of them demanded, 'The man asked you where you came from, mister! Who the hell are you?' This one was as wide as a locomotive across the shoulders and chest, wearing a damp, red-checked shirt bursting at the seams. Besides him there was a nervous-looking kid with yellow hair and two cross-belt-slung Colts and a darker, faintly Indian-looking man.

'Stoney Gordon's my name,' Cougar told them, his expression still all innocence. 'I figure we're all heading the same way. Did you say you've got coffee left? Seems I can smell it. Don't matter if it's cold.'

'We didn't say anything about coffee, or a word about which way we was riding,' the man with the beard said. The wind was blowing cold across the mesa, drifting bits of broken brush before it. The men encircling Cougar had gradually eased a little closer and they didn't seem quite as tense now, quite as likely to loose a shot on general principle. Still their eyes were wary, their jaw muscles clenched, fingers curled around the triggers of their guns.

'What'd you say your name was?' the barrel-chested man asked.

'I'm Stoney Gordon. There no reason for you to have heard of me, though.' Cougar moved easily to the dead camp fire and did indeed find a cold pot of coffee there. He drank the little remaining in it from the pot while the others exchanged glances. 'I didn't expect to find anyone up here. But it's good to be on high ground.'

'I don't trust those damned Apaches,' the man with the beard said. 'I ride high, camp high.'

'I don't trust them either,' Cougar said. 'Doesn't matter if we are all supposed to be on the same side.'

'He does know, Matt,' the blond kid said.

'Shut up! Where did you say you were heading, Gordon?'

'Trampas Ranch, like I reckoned you boys were. I figure I must be right on top of it, but I couldn't find it in the dark and rain. How about you?'

'We couldn't find it either,' the kid said.

'Shut up, Fiddler — we don't know who this hombre is.'

'I just told you,' Cougar said mildly. He put the coffee pot back and rose to his feet. 'I got a job with the people at Trampas. I figure you do too.'

'What kind of job?' the big man asked suspiciously.

'Me? I used to be in artillery long ago,' Cougar told him.

'When?'

'Long ago, friend.' He had already identified their Georgia accents and added ruefully, 'When we used to shoot at boys in blue uniforms.'

'That's not telling me much. Where was this?' the man with the beard asked, continuing to pursue the matter.

'A couple of places you might know,' Cougar said, removing his hat to wipe his hair back. 'Like Cross Keys, Vicksburg, Shiloh.'

'I was at Vicksburg,' the one with the beard, the one called Matt, said. 'I didn't see you.'

'I didn't see you either,' Cougar answered dryly. 'Me, I was up on the ridge with Johnston. I didn't see much of much but powder smoke for most of a month.'

'Ah, leave him alone,' the barrel-chested man said. 'He's OK, Matt. Why would anyone else be riding out here?' He holstered his Colt, to Cougar's relief.

Matt wasn't finished with him. He still held his rifle at the ready. 'You got to satisfy me a little more, friend.'

'I can try. Are you men out here working?' Cougar asked.

'That could be,' Matt answered hesitantly.

'Did they pay you like they paid me?' Cougar asked, and casually he slid the double eagles and the Prussian gold piece from the chamois purse he had captured. Matt stepped up to look at them by moonlight. 'They also sent me a little letter,' Cougar added with a grin, and he handed over the letter written in German.

'You can read this, can you?'

'No — I had to have a schoolteacher do that for me,' Cougar said, forced to invent some tale. The letter, he had assumed, was one constituting an introduction, assuring safe passage to its carrier. It didn't matter because it was obvious none of them could read the letter either. Now, however, even Matt was appeased.

'Sorry, Gordon,' he said. 'We've got to be cautious on this job. You can understand that.'

'I appreciate that,' Cougar answered. 'I'd have done the same thing in your place. Caution is about all that keeps a man walking around healthy these times.'

'What made you sign up for this job, Gordon?' the big man asked.

Again Cougar tried to judge where their sympathies lay. He tried saying, 'I figured it was my last chance to get back at those damned Yankees.'

The kid, Fiddler, at least laughed appreciatively. 'Me, I was too young,' Fiddler said. 'But I wasn't too young to watch them come and burn our house and our crops, to see my daddy come home a cripple.'

'I know,' Cougar said with what he judged to be the proper amount of sympathy. 'Anyway, that's what I'm here for. If things work out, I figure there'll be enough land for all of us.'

'For us and the foreigners?' Matt asked in a leading way.

'Them,' Cougar answered with a thin smile, 'I figure can be moved out later.'

'I like the way you think,' Matt said, and now he relaxed enough to smile.

'Spread out your bed, Gordon, and tomorrow we'll find that ranch.'

'Obliged to you,' Cougar said. Now, he knew, he had put his neck out a long way. But how else could he have solved the dilemma without getting himself shot up? Come tomorrow he would be forced to ride with these four into Trampas Ranch — he had no thought of attempting an escape in the night. That was folly. Perhaps riding in with a band of men could conceal his presence. The risk might not be as great as it appeared at first glance. Only Reineke could know who he was, only Reineke, and even he could not have known for sure that it was Cougar who had been stalking him the night before, or even that he was the target of a stalker. Unless circumstances brought them face to face with each other by pure chance, there was every reason for Cougar to think that he could infiltrate this army with impunity. At least for long enough to find Solon Reineke in some private place and finish matters.

Cougar rolled up in his damp blankets in the partial shelter of a knobby boulder and for a long time he watched the skies, the glow of the moon through sheer, shifting clouds. Then with a smile on his lips, he dozed off to sleep as the cold wind gusted.

Cougar's smile had not been a pretty smile. Solon Reineke wouldn't have liked it in the least.

15

Dawn broke in a dazzling array of colors soon overtaken by the brilliantly golden ball of the sun floating above the eastern horizon. The wild country came to life and the hills moved out of the concealing shadows of night. The five men were in the saddle and on their way an hour after dawn, the morning sun warm on their backs, the land already growing dusty as the porous desert sand greedily swallowed the rain that had fallen.

'How far do you think Trampas is, Matt?' the kid, Fiddler, asked.

'Just guessing, maybe five miles. It could be we're already on the ranch. I've no idea how big it is.'

The big man, whose name Cougar had discovered by now was Barkley, rode in gloomy silence. When Matt once prodded him, asking him why he was so dark-mooded all the time, he had answered, 'I just never really liked riding toward war, that's all.'

'Why do it, then?' Fiddler asked. The kid himself was eager to join the battle.

'It's all I can do, kid,' Barkley said, squinting at the young man from under the shadow of his hat brim. 'Damn me, that's just all I ever did learn to do.'

'I see smoke,' Cougar told them, and he lifted a pointing finger. Beyond a low row of green-clad hills smoke was indeed rising into the clear blue sky. It was probably from the camp of the foreign soldiers Cougar had seen the day before, for the fire was large. The Indians, Western men would have kept the fire small.

As they continued to ride down toward the valley floor, Cougar began to pick up sentries from the corners of his eyes, men standing on the low red bluffs and in canyon shadows, and he wondered if they were still hunting for him. He assumed they were just standing picket, and his own cover seemed adequate now that he was riding with a group of volunteers — but you just never knew.

The camp, by daylight, was much larger than he had estimated in the night. Besides the main buildings there were dozens of shacks thrown up along a gully, which was being used to collect trash, and farther on was a tent city he had not seen at all. Men in different uniforms, or no uniform at all, turned to watch them as they passed, dismissed them and got back to whatever they had been doing.

'Where now, I wonder?' Fiddler said.

'We'll ask somebody,' Barkley answered. By daylight Cougar could see now that the big man carried three rifles and two visible pistols, one slung over his saddle horn. Yeah, he was ready for war.

They rode past a thin, slow-walking man, who searched them with suspicious eyes and Barkley bellowed at him: 'Where do we find whoever's in charge of this army?'

'They expectin' you?' the thin man

asked, rocking back on his heels, thumbs hooked into his gunbelt.

'They asked for us; they got us,' Barkley shot back.

'There's a man named McQueen. Acting sergeant. He's in the barracks yonder,' the thin man said, pointing, and they started that way, the horses walking slowly, heads down. The porch of the barracks Cougar had seen on the previous night was now crowded with men repairing leatherwork, cleaning weapons, whittling, and playing cards. They were a rough-looking, competent-appearing bunch of men.

Pulling their horses up before the porch, Barkley shouted out, 'McQueen!' and after a minute a rangy, balding, blond man appeared on the porch, hatless, and wearing a handgun strapped around the back of his hip. There was a scar straight across his left eye and an impatient manner about him.

'I'm *Sergeant* McQueen,' the man said, turning his head to spit.

'Well, I'm Graham Barkley — I'm

carrying no rank that matters anymore. These are my friends. We was sent for.'

'Who says?' McQueen asked belligerently. Cougar saw a flush creep up the back of Barkley's neck as his irritation mounted.

'*I* say it — you just heard me, didn't you?'

The two men disliked each other at first sight. Cougar was determined to be silent and let Barkley take all the heat and hold everyone's attention. A few eyes lifted inquisitively from the porch. Some were merely curious, others faintly amused, some coldly savage. One man tilted back in a chair against the wall of the barracks, slapped the cylinder of the Colt Walker he had been cleaning back in sharply, and placed the big revolver too visibly on his lap.

'Take it easy, partner. I just don't know you, that's all,' McQueen muttered, trying to maintain the aura of rank that he believed he had.

'Well,' Barkley told him gruffly, 'we're

here and I'm not riding back to Arkansas just 'cause you don't know me.'

'You got a letter?' McQueen asked suspiciously.

'Why, damn you . . . ' Barkley began, sputtering a little.

'I got mine handy, Graham,' Cougar said lazily, and he leaned down from the buckskin to hand the German letter to McQueen. It was obvious that he also did not read the language, but he had seen a few of the letters before.

'All right,' McQueen said, handing the letter back after a minute he dragged out intentionally.

'You boys got specialties?'

'Explosives,' Graham Barkley answered peevishly.

'You?' McQueen asked Cougar.

'Artillery.'

'OK. How about the rest of you?'

'I could be called a sniper,' Matt said. He wasn't taken with McQueen either. 'Or a squirrel hunter — whichever you need most.'

'You?' McQueen asked Fiddler irritably.

'I'm whatever they want. I kill,' he said, and before any of them could blink he had unlimbered both of the Colts he wore and with fluid movements fired four .44-caliber rounds, all of which hit a hanging lantern above the porch as the soldiers dove for cover. Fiddler just sat there grinning. 'That's what I do,' the kid said.

'You don't do it here, damn you!' someone shouted and Fiddler just shrugged, holstering his guns.

'All right.' McQueen was obviously flustered. 'Do you men have a tent with you?'

'No.'

'You can find one at the log building there. That's our supply shack. Stake out a spot for yourselves along the wash, and stay there. No wandering in and out of camp. Also,' he warned them, 'make camp with the Americans. Stay the hell away from the Prussians and the Mexicans.'

'We'll do that,' Barkley said. He leaned across the withers of his horse and McQueen, still obviously agitated, snapped at him, 'You got a question?'

'Yeah. Two. When do we fight and when do we get paid?'

'You'll be told,' McQueen said and Barkley spat and turned his horse away from the barracks, the others following him as he wove through the oak grove Cougar was familiar with from his excursion the night before. They passed behind the big stone house and reached the wash where a few small camp fires burned and men, some in their underwear, some fully dressed, hung around impatiently. All of them — no matter what state of dress they happened to be in — were wearing guns.

They picked up a four-man tent from the supply hut and continued on their way. Barkley was still prickly on the subject of McQueen. 'I did not like that little son of a bitch,' he said twice to them.

No one answered. They pitched the tent, watered their horses at a pond, and picketed them out to graze.

Cougar had tossed his bedroll into the tent and started to spread it out when the popping sounds of guns being fired startled him and, snatching up his Spencer, he rushed out of the tent. Other men were dashing helter-skelter toward the sounds. They emanated from the dry wash, and there they came upon Fiddler banging away with practice shots from both pistols. Men cursed and turned back toward their activities, but Cougar stayed to watch.

He had heard stories about men shooting that way, but he had always taken them with a pinch of salt. As much as he had been around he had never seen a real fast-draw man or a man who could do equal damage with either hand. Now he was seeing it as he watched Fiddler. It was uncanny, was what it was. Both guns banging away, and if the kid missed a single one of the tin cans he had set up to shoot at,

Cougar didn't see it.

When Fiddler had to quit to reload, Cougar slid down the sandy bluff to join the blond man in the river bottom.

Fiddler turned and grinned, slapping the loading gate on his right-hand revolver shut before he holstered it.

'Well?' the kid asked, a hint of approval-seeking in his voice.

'Good shooting,' Cougar acknowledged.

'No better than 'good'?'

'You know how good you are, Fiddler — why ask me?' Cougar replied.

The kid shrugged. 'One day this talent just came to me, you know? Hell, I'd been shooting all my life, but something special came to me. Something other men don't have. I don't think about pulling the hammers back, Gordon. I don't think about aiming half the time. It just happens when I cut loose . . . I don't really think I can miss. Ever.'

Just keep on thinking that, kid, Cougar thought. We all miss.

He looked up as they both heard the sound of approaching hoofbeats and then looked quickly away and down, his heart rapping heavily against his rib-cage.

Solon Reineke! He and that little popinjay in the blue uniform were just above them on their mounts. Reineke's eyes slid across Cougar, narrowing in puzzlement. It was the look we give someone when we run across them in a place they have no business being. For just a moment recognition seemed to flash in his eyes, but all Reineke said was:

'We don't shoot in camp. Are you new here?'

'Brand new,' Fiddler answered, hands on his hips, confident smile on his lips.

'All right, then — but no more of that, soldier,' Reineke told him, and then, after the briefest hesitation as he seemed to consider Cougar again, he turned his horse and the two men rode out of camp toward the south, a body of six men falling in behind them.

'Who was that?' Fiddler asked.

'I've no idea,' Cougar lied. 'Must be one of the bosses.'

Cougar wiped his damp palms on his trouser legs. His mouth was dry. He felt that he had been only a hair's breadth from death. When would something in the back of Reineke's mind nudge realization? Something had to be done and it had to be done now. He meant to dog Reineke's trail and wait for his chance.

Without seeming to be in a hurry, Cougar said goodbye to Fiddler, walked back to where the buckskin was picketed and led it to the tent, where he saddled up.

Barkley came out and watched in silence, saying only, 'I thought you'd be tired of riding by now.'

'I'm tired of this camp already, that's all. I'm not good at sitting around. I'm going to take a look around and maybe bring back some venison for us, with any luck.'

'Me,' Barkley said, stroking his beard,

'I'm going to sleep. I figure we'll all be doing enough riding soon.'

'I hope you're right about that,' Cougar said, swinging aboard the buckskin. 'Me, I get fidgety when there's too much waiting to do.'

Cougar trailed out slowly, but he was still close enough to Reineke and his bunch that someone in the camp called out, 'Kind of lagging, aren't you?' as he passed.

Cougar grinned. 'I'll catch up. There's plenty of time.'

Then he picked the buckskin up into a trot and started following Reineke's tracks. That was in itself a dangerous game, but it seemed unlikely that they would be looking for someone from their own camp to follow them out on to the desert. Once in open country, tracking without being detected would be much more difficult. But then, Cougar didn't need to ride on their heels to follow them.

He already knew where they were headed: toward the White Mountains and General Crook's camp. There was absolutely nothing else in that direction. What Solon Reineke's plan was he had no idea, but that did not matter either — he had Reineke as good as in his sights now.

Cougar was so intent on his quarry that he never saw the lone rider fall in behind him and begin to follow along.

Cougar kept his distance from the men riding ahead of him. He wouldn't make any sort of move until dusk if he decided to do it then. He was now curious as to what Solon Reineke was really up to. Could he accomplish more by maintaining his distance? Cougar didn't know. He only knew that the desert was long and the day hot, a few sullen white clouds drifting aimlessly across the Arizona skies, occasionally staining him with their shadows as the big buckskin horse paced out effortlessly across the red-sand plateau.

The mesas appeared like a barrier reef lined up against the western skies. Still, here and there, Cougar passed ponds formed by the recent rain, and in these the rushes were already greening, and around them circled deer and coyotes, cougar and badgers ignoring one another. Only water mattered to each of them just then.

Still, as the sun rose higher, the small company of soldiers headed by Solon Reineke filed across the desert bleakness.

And still behind Cougar, undetected, the lone rider followed in his hoofprints. The long desert after the rain was flooded with brief, frantic life: new flowers, fresh water, new green budding things.

Soon it would be flooded with the blood of sudden death.

16

Dusk came early, a deep, velvet presence across the fading land. The soldiers led by Reineke set up camp, and from the shadows of the twilight, the hunter watched them. Now, he thought, was the time to take Reineke. Just now.

Cougar half-lifted himself from behind the screening brush where he had sheltered and glanced back into the arroyo where he had tied his buckskin horse, and when he did, from out of nowhere the man's body flung itself through the dusky light and collided roughly with his.

He felt the slap of muscles against him, saw the wild eyes and the deadly flash of steel. Cougar's fending arm came up as he was being driven backward, and he slammed his elbow forward into the man's throat. The attacker choked and buckled up, but still he slashed out at Cougar with his hunting knife. Cougar kicked him away, his boot landing solidly against the man's belly, and he rolled aside, coming to his feet as he reached for his own bowie, slipping it from the sheath at the back of his belt.

Still neither man had made a sound beyond the grunts of effort, the panting as their lungs strained for breath. Cougar knew the job had to be done quickly and silently — Reineke's camp was within easy earshot and he couldn't afford to stir it up. He could not allow the Apache to destroy his stalking game.

The Indian came in and Cougar slapped the man's knife hand away, backheeling him at the same time so that the Apache fell on his back, the breath rushing out of him.

Then Cougar was on the Indian warrior like a big cat mauling. The point of his bowie was already at the Apache's throat when a small curse escaped his throat and he involuntarily held back on the deadly thrust.

Damn it all. It was Fox Ring!

Quiet Star's husband . . . Images flashed through his mind: teaching the doe-eyed girl to read; her shyly handing him the medallion he still wore; her kicking and scratching as he took her back to the reservation; her eyes glowing when she watched him secretly; the heat of her anger that day that she believed General Crook had provided the reservation Indians with bad meals.

'Damn all!' Cougar muttered. This was the man Quiet Star loved, the man she had married. Now, angry and incapacitated, Fox Ring was watching Cougar with savage eyes, waiting for the thrust of the big man's knife.

Cougar still did not move. His great muscles were locked in indecision. Finally, angrily, he reversed his grip on the knife and slammed the butt of the handle against the side of Fox Ring's temple, and the Apache sagged into silent unconsciousness, groaning as he fell.

It wasn't much of a sound, that muffled groan, but it seemed to catch the attention of the men in Solon Reineke's camp. Cougar saw two of them come to their feet and reach for their holstered pistols.

'What was that?' It was Reineke who spoke. Now they were alerted, damn all. Cougar looked toward them through the twilight gloom in frustration. Then he slid down into the arroyo to work his way toward his horse. Behind him someone spoke again.

'Better take a look up there.'

Cougar heard men breaking through the brush toward the ridge where Fox Ring lay. He swung aboard the buckskin, but did not start the horse immediately away. He could hear more sounds of a furious, rapid search and then someone announced, 'Damn! It's Fox Ring, Solon!'

'Who could have . . . ?' someone asked and then Reineke spoke again.

'I know who it was,' he said. 'Goddammit, he's out here. I thought it was him I saw. Now I know. He's *here* and he's tracking.'

Cougar turned his horse carefully and walked it across the muffling sand of the arroyo bottom. They would not come searching for him in the darkness. This he knew. Reineke was not that stupid.

The game had changed. Now each knew the other one was here, ready to do harm on sight. Now, Cougar decided, he would have to take a different tack. He was away, merged with the shadows, but before he was completely gone, he heard Solon's whispery voice speaking across the distance between them: 'I know who it was.' Then, even more softly, he added, 'Damn you, Cougar. Damn you to hell, big man.'

*   *   *

Suddenly the fort was there. It was nothing much to see across the distances; a small log structure with two blockhouses staining the desert with shadow, sharpened palisades and a limp flag on its pole. Despite its unprepossessing aspect, it was a comfort to Ellen White. They had been seeing Indians all too frequently, their intentions always in doubt. Usually there were only small bands, and sometimes only a hint of their presence on the horizon where their signal smoke rose, but she had not forgotten the sight of her father's mutilated body and knew well that something similar, if not worse, could happen to the three of them as well.

Dallas McGee had given a whoop when he had first spotted the fort and said, 'Finally!' with obvious relief.

'What do you care?' D'Arcy had asked. 'You won't be there long enough for it to matter.'

'One night in a bunk will suit me,' Dallas answered. 'Don't tell me that you're riding right back out, Calvin?'

'I have to once the girl is settled,' D'Arcy answered grimly and again Ellen realized that there was much more going on than she had been made privy to.

'That means I am too, I guess,' McGee grumbled. His dream of a night in an army cot, safe from the hazards of a desert camp under a roof, had just gone up in smoke.

They passed through the main gate under the close scrutiny of the guards and crossed the yard toward the commanding officer's office. The fort, Ellen noticed, was crowded not only with soldiers, but with settlers' wagons and 'blanket' Indians who had come there for more protection as times grew more perilous beyond the gates.

All three of them swung down in front of the headquarters building and, stamping the dirt from his boots, dusting his jeans as best he could, D'Arcy entered, Ellen and Dallas McGee electing to wait outside, standing in the shade beneath the awning above the porch.

The first sergeant was unfamiliar to D'Arcy. He sat behind his desk, sleeves rolled up over thick, wiry-haired fore-arms, his flushed face sagged into a bulldog expression. In the corner a duty corporal shuffled papers, absently glancing at D'Arcy.

'What do you want?' the sergeant asked tiredly.

'I want to see the acting CO, whoever that might be.'

'He ain't here.'

'Where is he?'

The sergeant's eyes narrowed. He was one of those career soldiers who feels only contempt for civilians, who-ever they were. 'I don't know. In his quarters, maybe.'

'Look,' D'Arcy said, feeling the heat rise in his face, 'this is very important, Sergeant.'

'I know — everything is important. Any time someone walks in here it's important . . . to them,' the sergeant answered indifferently.

'I need to find General Crook and fast,' Calvin D'Arcy told him.

'I can't help you.'

'Damn you!' D'Arcy's temper broke loose. 'You tell me where the acting CO is or when you expect him back, and tell me now, or — '

The door opened behind D'Arcy at that point and he swiveled his head to see the captain enter through the door, framed by bright sunlight from outside. The sergeant had begun to rise from behind his desk. D'Arcy and the officer stared at each other for a moment.

'Pointer?' D'Arcy asked in surprise.

The captain grinned in response. 'Calvin D'Arcy, well, damn my eyes!'

The captain stepped forward and the two men shook hands. The sergeant asked uncertainly, with a shadow of belligerence in his voice, 'Do you know this man, sir?'

'I sure do,' Captain Pointer answered. 'One of the damndest scouts we ever had around here, and a hell raiser of the first order.'

'Not as much of one as Lieutenant Pointer was in those days,' D'Arcy pointed out. Pointer had gained a bar on his epaulets and a few pounds around the waist, but he looked much the same as he had in those earlier times.

'Those were all unfounded rumors!' Pointer laughed. 'What in the world brings you back out here, D'Arcy?'

'Can we talk in your office, sir?' D'Arcy inquired, nodding toward the closed office door.

'It's that important?' the officer asked, eyes narrowing.

'It's that important, sir.'

Pointer shrugged. 'All right. Come on in, Calvin.'

He led the way into a darkly furnished office with crossed sabers and a flag on the wall. Behind a leather-topped desk, Pointer settled into a chair. The brass sign on the desk in front of him read, 'General George Crook, Commander'. The captain gestured D'Arcy to a chair and he too sat, placing his hat on his crossed knee.

'What is it then, Calvin?' the captain

asked, glancing at the closed door to the office.

'I've got to get to Crook.'

Pointer smiled thinly, pondered it and then shook his head. 'I can't reveal his position, not even to you. You know how the general feels about security.'

'Yes, sir. I know very well.' D'Arcy leaned forward intently, 'But this is more important than even the general's need for security, Pointer.' He reached into his shirt pocket then and took out the letter wrapped in oilskin. He handed the letter to the doubtful young officer. 'This man wants me to find Crook, Captain Pointer.'

Pointer read the letter and then reread it, his eyebrows drawing together in astonishment. 'What's this about, D'Arcy?'

'That, I can't tell even *you*, sir.'

'Fine, the two us of with orders not to reveal information — mine from Crook, yours from President Grant himself. What are we to do?'

'I could track the general myself, sir,

but it would take far too long. This is extremely urgent.'

Captain Pointer sighed through his mouth and tapped his fingers on Crook's desk. Finally he asked, 'Can you tell me what is at stake here, D'Arcy?'

'Everything, sir,' was D'Arcy's answer.

It was a full minute before Pointer came to his decision and answered, 'All right, I'll show you his line of travel and bivouac sites.' He stood, his face revealing lingering uncertainty, and went to a map hanging on the wall. 'He planned to follow the White River, ascend to Pinetop, and by means of Silver Creek to Cottonwood. That's here,' he said, tapping the map, 'if it is not familiar to you. It's there that he expects to find Fox Ring's home camp. If you were to ride due south you should be able to reach it as soon if not sooner than the general. But it's a bad ride, D'Arcy.'

'I know it. I've been that way before. But it's a ride I have to make, sir.'

'Can you make it, Calvin?' the officer asked. His eyes went to D'Arcy's arm, which hung limply by his side. 'I didn't want to say anything, but it's obvious that your arm is just about useless.'

'I can ride with one arm,' D'Arcy said defensively and the captain nodded thoughtfully.

'If you say so. All I can say,' he told the scout with some trepidation, 'is that this had damned well better be as important as you're making out. Any interference could cause Crook's entire plan to capture Fox Ring to go wrong. He would not be happy with me. With us. You could get yourself chewed out in a way you never dreamed possible; I could get my tail court-martialed for having given the general's plan up.'

'It's important enough to risk all,' D'Arcy assured him, 'even if Fox Ring escapes. That will seem a very minor defeat in the face of the overall picture.'

'I hope to God you're right,' Pointer said.

'Sir?' D'Arcy asked, changing subjects. 'Is the general's wife still on post?'

'No, she has gone East to stay with relatives for the time being. Why do you ask?'

'You sir — are you still married?'

'Of course.' Pointer was frowning again. 'Why would you ask me a question like that?'

'The thing is,' D'Arcy answered with a sheepish grin, 'I've got a single woman in tow, and she needs a place to stay for a while. The Apaches killed her father, a man named White who was coming out here to sign on as company surgeon.'

'Damn! That leaves us in a fix.' Pointer sat down again. 'I knew this Dr White was due to arrive; we needed him. His daughter . . . we can put her up for the time being, I suppose. I was happy to see you when first we met, Calvin, but you seem to have brought a load of trouble and bad news with you. Is there anything else I should know about that you haven't told me?'

'Yeah,' D'Arcy said, grinning as he put his hat on and started toward the door to the commander's office. 'Cougar's coming.'

★   ★   ★

Evening settling across the long desert found Fox Ring sitting apart from his men, on a low, rocky knoll. The land was flushed red with blood tones as the sun died, returning to its night-time home. There were deep-purple shadows in the canyons; the mesas were a deep blue. A slight phantom breeze moved restlessly across the land.

Fox Ring was deep in thought. The Apache warrior aimlessly rubbed two small stones together, looking toward the distant army post. They had blown their bugle once at sundown and lowered their striped banner. They would not be riding out again on this night.

Fox Ring had no fear of the cavalry, though he respected them. He did not even despise these white men who had come from over the seas, wishing to build their own new nation. They would fail, Fox Ring knew. For now, they were useful with their supplies and weapons. The Indian did not fear the men who hated him for his race, and there were many of them among the whites. They were all nothing — yapping pups rushing here and there.

No. He had seen one man who did trouble him riding into the fort that evening. He bothered Fox Ring because he was more than a soldier — a soldier fights for pay. These foreign opportunists fought for land and wealth. Some of his enemies fought simply out of hatred.

This man, the returning man, fought only out of a sense of obligation, and he would not quit until that sense had been satisfied. He was the sort of warrior to be most feared.

Carroll Cougar had returned.

We do hope that you have enjoyed reading this large print book.

Did you know that all of our titles are available for purchase?

We publish a wide range of high quality large print books including:
Romances, Mysteries, Classics
General Fiction
Non Fiction and Westerns

Special interest titles available in large print are:
The Little Oxford Dictionary
Music Book, Song Book
Hymn Book, Service Book

Also available from us courtesy of Oxford University Press:
Young Readers' Dictionary
(large print edition)
Young Readers' Thesaurus
(large print edition)

For further information or a free brochure, please contact us at:
Ulverscroft Large Print Books Ltd.,
The Green, Bradgate Road, Anstey,
Leicester, LE7 7FU, England.
Tel: (00 44) **0116 236 4325**
Fax: (00 44) **0116 234 0205**

SPARROW'S GUN

Abe Dancer

Before setting off in pursuit of his father's murderers, Will Sparrow must learn how to handle a gun . . . Miles away from home, he plans his reprisal while working as a stable-boy. But then Laurel Wale happens along, and Will discovers his intentions aren't quite as clear-cut as he thought . . . Meanwhile, his mother has settled down nearby with one of the territory's most important citizens. She wants nothing more than peace — but nothing is going to deter Will from his fateful objective.

BLACKJACKS OF NEVADA

Ethan Flagg

Five years in prison have given Cheyenne Brady plenty of time to dwell on revenge after being left for dead during a hold-up by the Nevada Blackjacks. Upon his release Brady joins up with an old prospector, Sourdough Lamar; together they head for Winnemucca and the prospect of honest work. But when Brady's old gang, led by Big-Nose Rafe Culpepper, plans to rob the town's bank, Cheyenne is accused of masterminding the hold-up. Can he extricate himself from once again sinking into a life of crime?

INCIDENT AT FALL CREEK

D. M. Harrison

As Charles Gilson's line of employment usually involves wanted dodgers and a sawn-off shotgun, when he receives news of an inheritance, he is determined to make a fresh start. But Gilson has competition for the money: Theodore Alden has charged his lawyer with securing it by fair means or foul. With everyone, including Town Marshal Hardy, against Gilson, the odds seem stacked against him — it will take more than a few bullets to secure what is rightfully his . . .

WHITE WIND

C. J. Sommers

Spuds McCain is convinced the White Wind brings disaster to all those who sense its message. Hobie Lee is sceptical. But bad things do happen to the Starr-Diamond Ranch — Hobie is hoodwinked and ambushed into trouble when his charge, Ceci Starr, disappears on a trip to town. The White Wind blows away the rest of his common sense as he determines to restore the reluctant Ceci to her father: it will take a maelstrom of death and double-cross before it blows itself out and Hobie can find peace.

DIABLO

Chuck Tyrell

On the streets of Diablo jobs are scarce, tempers roil, and dead men are stripped almost before they hit the ground. But Shawn Brodie needs to collect $3,000 for Tin Can Evans, and that amount of money can cause epic problems for a man in a hell of a town such as this. With a host of dangerous men walking its streets, it's only a matter of time before the fuse is lit that threatens to blow Diablo all to Hell . . . which may be where it belongs.

BACK FROM BOOT HILL

Colin Bainbridge

After finding himself inside a coffin on the way to Boot Hill, Clay Tulane wants answers. Whilst local towns-folk Miss Winona and the boy Pocket help him piece together the story of how he got there, Tulane finds himself drawn into a violent struggle against local landowner Marsden Rockwell and his Bar Nothing outfit, who want to take over the neighbouring Bar L. As tension mounts, the search for the truth throws up many more ques-tions . . .